BLOOD IN THE PAST

Jordanna East

FIRST EDITION
Blood Read Press
Collingswood, NJ 08108

ISBN: 978-0-9895810-1-1

For my husband, Justin. I can't imagine where I would be without you, let alone where my writing would be. You pushed me when I wanted to fall down and wither away. Do me a favor, never stop pushing.

For my friend, Jillian. You left too soon and now I like to imagine you're playfully taunting the people below you, making them believe you're sitting in a tree, when you're really sitting in the window behind it. I'll join you there one day. We'll taunt them together.

1
Barren Platform.

JILLIAN GAZED AT the family across from her. Two young girls pranced around their parents. They stumbled with the swaying and lurching of the train, the beads at the ends of their braids clattering like marbles in a satchel. The father lifted one daughter onto his lap while the mother straightened the other's dress. The family's skin was the same syrupy brown as Jillian's, but the similarities ended there. Though the girls' cheekbones were high and rounded like hers, they weren't hidden behind years of despondence. Jillian smiled at them, and the mother nodded politely. Before Jillian could entertain another somber thought, her roommate, Mel, elbowed her hard in the ribs.

"Get up. We're gonna miss our stop."

"I know, Mel." Jillian's voice was so soft Mel probably hadn't heard her. Jillian wasn't used to being heard anyway.

They grabbed their belongings from the floor, nestled between their feet. Jillian had taught Mel to put her feet through the straps so no one could shoot through the car and snatch her bag before dashing out the closing doors. Mel had scoffed until she'd seen it done to another passenger on the way home from a concert one night.

Mel swung from pole to pole through the subway car toward the exit, unaware of her surroundings, while Jillian marched behind her. Though Jillian would never admit it, she envied Mel's devil-may-care nature. The doors slid open before them, then closed with a thud behind them. Before the train rushed off, Jillian glanced back at the happy, nuclear family and wondered if they were heading home after eating out at a family restaurant. Perhaps even celebrating the girls' good report cards. She shoved her hands deep in her pockets to keep herself from waving.

Jillian made use of her long legs to catch up to her roommate. "You know, I wait for you after class. The least you could do is wait for me once in a while." Her usually meek volume elevated only slightly, but her annoyance was still palpable.

"I don't need you to wait for me. I keep telling you that." Mel popped her gum loudly. The echo shot throughout the platform. "What were you staring off at anyway? I'm too hungry for your damn subway daydreams, kiddo."

Jillian cringed when Mel called her "kiddo." Mostly because Mel, as the outsider, the naive one, was not in a position to condescend. The girl possessed all the markings of someone trying to hide her true vulnerability. Her harsh face, framed by a short, angled haircut, was peppered with piercings and darkened with severe eyeliner. If anyone called her by her full first name, Melody, she'd stare daggers through their face. Her roommate was right about one thing, though: Jillian didn't need to wait for her. It wasn't as if they were friends. They had virtually nothing in common. Yet, Jillian thought waiting was the polite thing to do. Their classes ended at almost the same time, and they were going to the same place. Still, maybe she wouldn't wait for Mel next week.

Jillian rolled a scrunchie off of her wrist and tried her best to smooth her long, thick hair into a ponytail. Although a crisp, barely-spring evening awaited them above ground, the subway platform felt humid, soupy even. The barren platform stretched out before them, peppered with steel columns scarred by chipped, peeling paint. Their classes ended after eight p.m. on Thursdays: too late for the rush-hour crowd, too early for the bar crowd. Jillian embraced the silence and inhaled the scent of cigarette butts and urine that reminded her of her childhood. She waited for Mel to make a sarcastic remark about the stench.

Mel's complaint never came.

As they approached the staircase to the street, a shadow darted around one of the columns and rushed toward them from the left, barely within Jillian's peripheral vision. She saw it a fraction of a second before Mel. The shadow stepped in front of them, blocking the stairs. Jillian's focus crept concentrically outward from the dull, steel barrel of the gun to the man's hooded face.

Jillian gasped, more out of surprise than fear. But Mel's scream echoed. Jillian nudged her roommate to quiet her. After a moment of shock and hesitation, they thrust their bags toward the man—just as a metallic *click* reverberated through the silence of the deserted subway platform.

"9-1-1, what's your emergency?"

"We were mugged on our way home from class," Jillian answered as she unlocked the door to their apartment, her voice as smooth and calm as her facial features. She watched Mel amble ahead of her, head straight to their futon, and cower into the corner of it. She brushed a sharp, black strand of hair from her forehead. Visibly quivering, tears streamed into the tissue she clutched with both hands. Jillian supposed a gun in the face would do that to anyone not from a big city. Mel came from a tiny speck on the map in Ohio before she

3

moved out to Philadelphia for grad school.

Jillian, on the other hand, had been robbed at gunpoint during her freshman year of college. As much as she'd loved her iPod, she handed it over without a word, along with her favorite shoulder bag. She remembered glaring at the gunman the entire time, daring him—no, willing him—to take the crime a step further. His eyes had widened in terror, unused to his prey challenging him. Jillian had even surprised herself that day, realizing then how damaged she was.

"Are either of you injured?" the dispatcher asked with only the slightest animation. Her dry, crackled voice snapped Jillian back to the present. Jillian placed an ungainly hand on her roommate's thigh to calm her; she could hardly hear the operator over Mel's sniveling.

"No, we're unhurt," Jillian replied. Mel's crying grew louder. She shoved her quaking hands under her thighs to steady them. Jillian wrapped an awkward arm around her, attempting to cradle her narrow shoulders. That was the closest they'd ever been, physically or otherwise.

The dispatcher asked several more questions, confirmed their address, and promised to send officers to take their statements. Jillian retreated to the kitchenette, thinking of her upcoming exam—a test on criminal psychology—and the notes she'd lost in the mugging. She chuckled at the irony.

In the living room, Mel returned to normal in phases, hardening before Jillian's eyes. Ten minutes passed, and Mel's shuddering body had almost stilled. She asked Jillian to retrieve the vodka from on top of the fridge, mumbling about how a swig of warm vodka would calm her nerves before the cops arrived. Always trying to appear badass, Jillian thought. *Unless a gun's pointed at her.*

Jillian tried not to roll her eyes at the facade as she reached for the liquor. "Only because you just quit smoking," she called over her shoulder.

"Just get me the damn vodka, Jill," Mel hissed, her voice hoarse from crying.

Jillian offered it to her by stretching over the back of the futon separating the sitting room from the kitchen. Mel snatched the bottle. Jillian dismissed Mel's abruptness and rounded the couch. She sat beside her, leaving a comfortable space between them; Jillian hoped to console Mel, but she didn't want to smother her. Mel swigged the vodka straight from the bottle and sat back, eyes closed. The only sound in the room was her deep exhale.

Jillian cut the silence first, but barely; her voice hovered near a whisper. "It's going to be hard to walk with someone behind you for a while, but you'll get over it."

The statement rang cold in the apartment, colder than she intended. Furthermore, she didn't know why she'd said it. If she wanted to use the ordeal to bond with Mel, she should have led with something more conventional, like a simple, *Are you okay?* Annoyed with herself, Jillian opened her mouth to better convey her sentiment, but Mel interrupted.

"What do you mean?" Mel shot up straight in her seat. "This has happened to you before?"

"Yes. Several years ago." As she often did when she felt uncomfortable, Jillian picked at imaginary hangnails, scraping each fingernail with another. She cleared her throat and continued, "It was no big deal, really. They don't hurt you as long as you give up your things. You saw how quickly that guy ran away after we gave him our bags."

"No big deal? No big deal!" Mel slammed the vodka bottle on the coffee table. "He had a gun pointed at our

5

faces! And he cocked it, like he was getting ready to shoot us! I can still hear that clicking noise."

During Mel's tantrum, some of the vodka splashed out of the bottle and sprayed Jillian's jeans. She wiped at the tiny, damp spots, concentrating more on her hands than her roommate. "Well, you shouldn't have screamed. You attracted too much attention. And you took too long to give him your stuff."

Mel stood up, scoffing loudly. "Um, yeah. You know what, Jill, I don't get you sometimes." Jillian watched her pace around the room. "Two years we've lived together, and I still don't fucking understand you, you know that?"

She gulped down some more vodka and stared at Jillian, her eyes hard despite the smudged, runny makeup staining her face. Jillian knew Mel was right. She'd never told her about her past, about how she grew up. Probably never would. In fact, Mel wouldn't even know Jillian's last name if it didn't appear on the mail. Still, Jillian wasn't about to explain that she was used to violence, used to having her belongings taken.

Jillian and Mel sat in silence until two officers showed up half an hour later. When the intercom hummed, Mel replaced the cap on the bottle of vodka and rolled it out of sight under the futon. Jillian ran downstairs to let them in. They were much older than Jillian and Mel, both graduate students at Temple University. The shorter one had graying, receding ash-blond hair, and the outline of his Kevlar vest beneath his shirt hardly covered his paunch. The taller one's hair utterly contrasted that of his partner's—thick and dark. A lovely complement to his complexion, Jillian thought. Their radios buzzed with officious-sounding chatter while the balding one asked the usual questions regarding their ordeal.

Mel did most of the talking, acting as though she'd recorded all the details of their attack. Jillian had largely dismissed the attacker's features. For Jillian, being mugged again just added another event to a long list of life's injustices. But for Mel, it was a life-changer. Jillian listened as her roommate rattled off imagined recollections of the mugger's clothes, the depth of his voice, and the appearance of his fingernails. She even thought she'd smelled a distinct odor on him. Jillian pressed her lips together to keep from snickering as Mel recalled smelling something other than the usual cigarette smoke and human waste. Jillian remembered reading in her criminal psychology text that witnesses often created erroneous details in order to escape their own subconscious feelings of helplessness, but was Mel serious?

Between the lines of questioning, the taller officer stole glances at Jillian. She chided her imagination; he wasn't checking her out. *Not here, not now.* But she failed to ignore his smiles, so out of place under the circumstances. She couldn't neglect his handsome face or the dangerous spark in his eyes. His olive-colored brow slanted forward just enough to cast a mysterious shadow over his dark eyes. Jillian fought to look away, especially once she noticed the officer's left hand.

The light in the room reflected off his wedding band as well as his badge. But Jillian felt warmed by the thought that she'd captured the man's attention, even if only in her imagination. *Even if he's married,* she mused, hoping her raised eyebrow went unnoticed.

When she chanced a second glance in the officer's direction, he winked. At least, she *thought* he winked. She lowered her eyes to his badge. The bold lettering read

"KYLE." Obviously a badge wouldn't display a first name, but she liked it as a last name. The other officer wrapped things up with Mel, so Jillian tried to think of a way to keep them there longer, if only for a few more minutes. She desperately wanted to know if Officer Kyle's advances were real or imagined.

The officers rose to leave. "We have coffee!" Jillian blurted, then winced. "I mean, would you guys like some coffee before you go?" *Way to not sound desperate.* Jillian could feel Mel's quizzical expression.

Officer Kyle stood a step behind his partner and said nothing. He looked at his feet, an action that failed to hide his smile. His partner answered politely, "No, thank you, ladies. We have to get back out there." He gestured toward the streets with a nod in the direction of the door. As if on cue, their radios blazed louder with codes and phrases foreign to Jillian.

She took a breath and tried again. "Okay, well, how does this work? Will you be back to follow up, or is there a number I—I mean *we*—can call if there's anything we've forgotten?" Her voice cracked once, prompting another sideways glance from her roommate. Officer Kyle reached over his partner's shoulder and handed a business card to Jillian, not Mel.

Calvin was his first name. Calvin Kyle. Jillian liked his first name even more than his last. Put together, they sounded like a smooth action movie hero, like James Bond or a character from *Mission Impossible* or *Ocean's 11*.

Calvin turned to Mel. "I'll be back to check on you both in a couple days." His voice rumbled deeply, yet buttery. His eyes sparkled, or so Jillian thought, when his gaze lingered on her a moment. She felt certain he spoke purely for her benefit.

2
Fought and Won.

CALVIN KYLE RETURNED two days later. Waiting had driven Jillian mad, but when she opened the door and saw him, her stomach melted. "Hi, uh, Officer." She was careful not to sound too obvious by using his name. "It's just me here at the moment. Mel's at class." She suspected he might be there for her though.

"No, I came to check on you both. I keep my promises."

Jillian ushered him in and led him upstairs to the apartment. The sticky stairs sucked at their soles, saving them from an uncomfortable silence. Or perhaps exacerbating it; Jillian couldn't be sure. When they reached her floor, she opened their door and he brushed past her, his uniform rustling against her T-shirt. Jillian felt her face warm as if the sun had crossed the threshold with him. "Okay, well, can I offer you some coffee or something?"

She watched from the kitchenette as Calvin made himself comfortable on the futon by moving aside throw pillows and textbooks. "So hospitable." He laughed, settled into the cushion, and twisted to face her. "Do you have lemonade?"

"Iced tea?"

"Perfect."

Jillian poured two glasses of iced tea. The ice cubes jostled and clinked as she approached him, her hands quivering with anticipation. She'd picked up on his attraction to her. He was there. In their apartment. To see her.

Now what?

Calvin shuffled through her note cards, then flipped through a few pages in her *Contemporary Clinical Psychology* text. "What are you studying?"

Jillian fumbled over the polite, yet personal, question. She managed to point at the cover of the textbook in his lap. Even if he was there for her, the absence of formalities unsettled her. She'd expected follow-up questions regarding the mugging, or even news that they'd caught the guy, however improbable that scenario. She felt more comfortable with subtle flirting than blatant advances. Then again, he'd only asked about her area of study. Finally, she found her words, speaking deliberately to keep from stuttering. "I'm getting my Master's in Clinical Psychology. This is my last year," she said, pointing to the cover of the textbook.

"Okay, that's it. I'm outta here." He half-stood with both hands up in mock concession. "I don't trust head doctors."

Jillian giggled into her hands. "Why does everyone say that?" She didn't even know which "everyone" she was referring to, but it felt like the right thing to say. With every shared laugh, Jillian knew his visit had little to do with the mugging.

Calvin shrugged. "No one likes to feel transparent, I guess. Makes them vulnerable. We all have secrets and private thoughts, experiences we'd rather keep to ourselves."

"That makes sense." Jillian failed to stop her gaze from falling to Calvin's wedding ring. He didn't seem to notice. "But that's part of the reason I chose that major." He slid closer and, with wide eyes, silently urged her to continue. She did but with solemnness to her tone. "I was a foster child. The good homes were few and far between. The bad homes were real-life nightmares, and no one wants to talk about their nightmares, right? I guess I just wanted to know why people are the way they are and do the things they do." He didn't say anything, and all of a sudden, Jillian felt a flush of embarrassment. "I'm sorry, I don't know why I'm telling you this. Mel doesn't even know——"

"It's okay. Let's talk about something else." Calvin placed his iced tea on the table. The glass slid an inch when the condensation met the cheap wooden surface. He interlaced his fingers and crossed his legs, imitating a cheesy, late-night talk show host. "So, Ms. Jillian, are you originally from Philly?"

"Yes, all parts. Northeast, West, South, and now North." Amused, Jillian heard her voice regain some of its luster. "As you can imagine, I moved around quite a bit."

"I see." He reached for his tea, took a sip, then returned the glass to the table. "Do you have a favorite?"

"Yeah—the one part I never lived in. Center City." Jillian exhaled, slightly betraying her lighthearted tone. *How can I love a place I've never spent much time in?* "City Hall, Love Park, Rittenhouse Square. And those towering buildings. They must have such spectacular views."

Jillian's eyes ignited with excitement. Her dream since making it to college was to have her own practice, perched high above the city in one of those sky-high office buildings. A small sigh escaped her lips.

"I'm sure you're right about that. So, what do you like to do in Center City? Suppose I were to take you somewhere, where would you like to go?"

"If you could 'take me somewhere?'" Jillian repeated, incredulous.

Calvin shrugged. "Sure."

Jillian let the space between them grow, scuttling to the

opposite end of the futon. "But...you're married?"

"I am. But, it's...complicated."

Jillian remained still, staring at her hands, begging them not to squirm. She'd known he was married. Fantasizing about his interest in her had been acceptable. But he *was* interested in her. That was different. That was wrong.

"Is my being married a problem?" he prodded, reaching to place a hand on her knee. Jillian withdrew but didn't have far to go. The armrest of the futon was already jutting into her side.

"I don't know. I, I think you should go." She brushed her thick, black hair behind her ears, dropped her hands to her lap, and fidgeted with her fingers. She didn't dare look at him, or she might change her mind.

Calvin stood without a word and saw himself to the door. Jillian sat motionless, but her mind juggled an innumerable flurry of questions. Maybe she shouldn't be so hasty. He was truly interested in her, and she was letting him walk away without knowing the whole situation. Perhaps he and his wife were in the process of separating. Perhaps his wife just wasn't a good person. Perhaps Jillian should find out, give him a chance.

When Calvin's hand reached for the knob, she jumped up and sprinted to the door, oddly compelled to act. Just as he was closing the door, Jillian pried it open. Calvin froze in the hallway, his back toward her. "The Franklin Institute! If I could go anywhere in Center City, I'd wanna go to the Franklin Institute." She demoted her cries to a whisper and added, "They just renovated the Planetarium." With that, Jillian closed the door softly before he could respond. She leaned against it and slid to the floor. *What did I just do?*

The next day, Mel banged on Jillian's bedroom door,

startling her awake. Grateful she didn't have class until noon, Jillian stretched her arms over her head and yawned. She'd tossed and turned all night over her attraction to a married man.

Before Jillian could say, "Come in," Mel entered the room. The effects of the mugging—dark circles and a down-turned mouth—were still on full display. "Hey, I found this pushed under the door. Has your name on it."

She tossed the envelope, and Jillian watched it soar across the room end-over-end. She caught it, and Mel left before she could look up. *Curious*, she thought. She didn't recognize the handwriting. She tore it open. Inside were two tickets to the Franklin Institute.

The ceiling twinkled and gleamed with the display of the stars and planets visible from that exact point on Earth, during that exact time of year. The generous air-conditioning sent a wave of crawling, shivering pinpricks over Jillian's bare arms. Calvin noticed and curled an arm around her. *What am I doing here?* she wondered, suddenly glad she sat to his right, so his wedding ring was out of sight for the moment. Jillian had no idea how to feel about their first date or the way he looked at her, listened to her. The feeling of being wanted flustered her. She had gone unwanted for far too long, her entire life even. Her father abandoned her pregnant mother, who then dumped Jillian in front of a hospital as an infant. Year after year, every household thereafter only took her in to collect a government paycheck. *Don't I deserve a real relationship, however complicated?*

After that afternoon at the Planetarium, Jillian fell for Calvin at a feverish pace. His desire felt so different from the foster homes, from the many schools and neighborhoods, and from the hundreds of faces that had passed in and out of her life, overflowing her world with rejection. Yes, Calvin was married. But for once, someone who already had a family wanted her—truly wanted her. So she held tight to Calvin Kyle.

They shared beds at hotels near the airport and candlelit dinners at restaurants in Jersey and Delaware. Their affair stretched from weeks to months. Calvin held doors for her and bought her trinkets. She'd never been in a similar relationship. Or any serious relationship, in fact. Calvin made her feel as though she had a voice, as though she was worth it. She didn't know what *it* was, but it made her feel alive. She could live a thousand lifetimes in a single day with Calvin. And she'd die a thousand deaths before she'd let him go. But one thing nagged at Jillian.

Calvin paid for their dinners in cash. She charged the rooms to her credit card, and Calvin reimbursed her. The arrangement pestered her somewhat. Keeping their relationship hidden was curious, since he insisted a separation between him and his wife was imminent. She'd asked him about it one night after he'd stuffed a handful of twenty-dollar bills into a black leather checkbook and handed it off to their waitress.

"Can't leave a paper trail for the little woman," he had joked.

"Yeah, about that." She'd looked up at him from the chocolate mousse she'd been toying with and frowned. "Where is what we have going if you're married?"

Calvin had answered with a garbled mess of words. The topic of leaving his wife remained the one blemish in his otherwise smooth demeanor, the one flaw in their romance. *I don't even know my rival's name*, she thought bitterly. But she knew his daughter's name: Lyla.

He spoke of her constantly: how she had graduated at the top of her class—pre-med at the University of Pennsylvania—and was currently serving her last year as a surgical resident at one of the more prestigious local hospitals. Calvin gushed with pride over her. Jillian assumed he didn't leave his wife because Lyla would be crushed.

But what about the crushing weight of his marriage on our relationship, Jillian often asked herself. But she held on. She held on against her better judgment because, for the first time, she had something—someone—to hold on to.

Early spring turned to late summer and it was their five-month anniversary. Jillian picked Calvin up at one of their meeting places. The tops of her brown breasts glistened in the rays of sun peeking through the sunroof. The strings to her bikini draped down from the back of her neck and tickled her collarbone.

"Happy anniversary, darling," she said with a beaming smile as Calvin stepped into the coupe.

He barely chuckled before pulling the door shut. Jillian leaned to her right for a kiss and met empty air instead. She disguised her humiliation by reaching into the glove compartment for a different pair of sunglasses, mumbling that they matched her bathing suit better. *Had Calvin forgotten about their anniversary?*

During the drive, Jillian tried to recall if Calvin had responded differently on anniversaries past. He hadn't really, so she assured herself he simply thought it was cute and youthful that she celebrated by month instead of just by year.

With her feet planted in the warm sand of Rehoboth Beach, she watched his skin deepening in the sun, his hair fluttering in the ocean breeze. Salt stained his legs from their earlier traipse near the approaching tide. Jillian cradled a book in her hand, but her lover's physique interested her far more than her novel. Rays of light glittered in the few gray hairs of his chest and sideburns. Sweat sparkled in the creases of his muscles. She desperately wished he'd turn to look at her so she could feel the warmth of his gaze coupled with the heat of the summer day. But facing the ocean, wearing a smirk, he appeared preoccupied.

Jillian followed his line of sight to see what had ensnared his attention. She scowled at the two girls her age frolicking in the surf topless. Calvin clearly enjoyed the view. The lifeguard's scolding shouts punctuated the thoughts bombarding her mind. Jillian found herself obsessed with everything that had happened that day. He had most certainly forgotten their anniversary. He hadn't spoken more than a dozen words during the three-hour car ride to Delaware, and he hadn't stolen a single glance at her since they'd arrived. Then he became distracted by other women. *Am I losing him?*

"Cal?" she called sweetly, trying to derail his focus.

He didn't answer. He continued to smile at the topless girls on the horizon.

"Cal!" she yipped, slamming the armrests of her beach chair.

Startled, he faced her, lowering his bronze-tinted sunglasses down to the tip of his nose. He squinted against the bright reflection of the sun off the sand.

"What's up, Jilly?"

Jillian tried not to speak through gritted teeth. Instead, she took a breath and forced a smile. "What are you thinking about, staring off into the ocean, without a care in the world?"

"Oh, just savoring the day."

Jillian affixed another fake smile and allowed silence to retake the moment. She focused on her breathing, aligning it to the rhythm of the crashing waves. Calvin had just lied to her. She tried to rein in her thoughts, to corral her feelings, but she found it impossible. She couldn't let him stray. She was his.

All her life, Jillian had been meek and submissive. She'd stayed in her place, whatever that was, and rarely spoke her mind. Not anymore. She exhaled through pursed lips and gripped the armrests, willing her fingers to convey strength rather than anxiety. "Cal, when are you leaving your wife?"

"We've talked about this." He sighed, still looking straight ahead, though the girls had reunited themselves with their bikini tops. "It's not the right time just yet."

"But there *is* a right time? One hopefully just around the corner?"

"Jill, my wife and I got married very young, basically right out of high school. We thought we were in love, and maybe we were. Then she got pregnant and we had Lyla, and we realized that what we thought we had was never there. Or it was and it was gone. The whole thing is very cliché, I'm sure, but the truth is we've been living virtually separate lives ever since. And I'm sorry, but I just can't pinpoint an exact date when we'll finally part ways. Do you understand?"

"I understand that you didn't answer my question. You do plan on leaving her, don't you?" Jillian winced when she heard her voice revert to its usual passive tone.

"I thought I answered your question." His voice was stitched with annoyance. "Look, can we not talk about this today? It's our anniversary."

Jillian fumed. Earlier he'd forgotten their little monthly milestone, and then he was using it against her. Was he testing her? Did he want her to fight for his attention, for his love? She could do that. She'd caught his eye months ago, and she could do it again.

"I'd like to go," she said coyly, placing a hand on his arm.

"Really? We still have a few more hours—"

"I know, but...The lifeguard has left for the day and most of the beachgoers have left as well..."

Jillian let her voice trail off and stood. The wind tossed her long ponytail over her shoulder and whirled sand around her mahogany curves. She leaned in close to Calvin, her breasts nearly spilling out of the triangles of her top. "Follow me," she said in a breathy whisper.

She clasped his hand and led him toward the wooden boardwalk. When they neared the ramp, she redirected him—*under* the boardwalk. Before he knew what happened, she kissed him hard and fast, devouring the windswept salt on his lips, falling with him to the soft sand. Unlike out in the open sun, the darkness provided cooler sand that conformed to their writhing bodies.

The wooden planks above rattled with the footsteps of passersby, blanketing any trace of their grunts and moans. The little sunlight that forced its way through the hurried crowd above the boards cast dancing cheetah spots of shadow across their sand-speckled, near-naked bodies.

Jillian threw her head back with pleasure. She'd fought and won, pushing herself to the forefront of Calvin's mind once more. She was his, and she was there to stay.

The following week, Jillian met Calvin in an alley near the

pub he and his colleagues frequented following their shifts. Calvin's early morning patrol shift had just ended, and he'd wanted to discuss the arrangements for one of their usual hotel trysts. The sun shone, but shadows dampened the alley. Only a few rays of sunshine accompanied them. Calvin spoke to her with an unusually firm tone; it sounded overly dour compared to the jovial man she'd come to know.

"So, we'll meet at the hotel at eight," he said. "Room 216. I memorized your Visa, so I made the reservation for us." He opened the door to his police cruiser, hopped in, and rolled down the window.

Jillian leaned into the car and watched her lover's eyes creep downward to her low-cut tank top. She kissed him deeply, the way she always did, but he pulled back. Just a little.

"Some of the guys still think you're an informant."

She pouted. "I thought you told them about me."

"I did, just not all of them—"

"By the way, I've been trying to call you since Delaware, baby." Jillian spoke in a coquettish tone, giddy to spill her news right then, but Calvin cut her off, nodding curtly.

"Listen, I want to talk about *us* tonight, Jilly."

Jillian's heart flip-flopped. *Finally!* That was what she had waited months for. Lyla was more than an adult and about to complete her last year of residency. In fact, she'd just moved into her own apartment. Calvin could finally leave his wife. Plus, this would be the perfect time to share her exhilarating news! *But why doesn't Calvin look as thrilled as I feel?*

Jillian craned into the car to give him another quick peck on the lips. Calvin said goodbye and headed home to catch up on some sleep—in the bed he still shared with his wife.

Driven by curiosity, and perhaps a bevy of other emotions, Jillian tailed him to his cobalt-blue, two-story townhouse.

The serene neighborhood on the outskirts of Philly intrigued her. She wanted so badly to be a part of it, and she even imagined Calvin returning home from work to *her*, greeting *her* with a kiss. Jillian wondered if she would move in with him or if he'd leave the house to his wife so they could start anew in their own house. Soon she would know. Maybe even after that night's talk.

Jillian arrived at the Atlantic City hotel early. She draped herself in a silk negligee—a gift from Calvin—and lit several gardenia candles. She always used a gardenia-scented conditioner, and Calvin had mentioned when they first met that he liked the way her hair smelled. In fact, he'd described the smell as "divine." Jillian shivered with anticipation as she ordered a bottle of champagne from room service—she didn't think a single glass would hurt—and sprawled across the king-sized bed to await her lover.

Calvin lumbered through the door well after eight. He didn't even spare a glance at Jillian. Instead, he circled the room and extinguished each candle with his thumb and forefinger. Finally, he perched on the edge of the bed and stared at her. Jillian didn't budge. Even holding the champagne flutes, she fought the urge to fuss with her hands under his scrutiny. He got up, turned up the lights as bright as they could go, and returned to his spot on the bed.

"Jillian, I've asked you several times not to call my house."

She sat up. Are we not about to have the talk I've looked forward to all day? The talk I've longed for the past five months?

Calvin continued. "I think we should stop seeing each

other. At least for a while."

"Baby, no." Jillian's voice fluttered, like her heartbeat. Her mind swam for a way to fix things. "You're right, I shouldn't call. I promise I won't. It's just that—"

"It's too late, sweetheart. My wife knows something's up. And now she's confided in my daughter and...I just need to be home with my family and set things straight, you know? We have to cool it for a while."

"You had to get us a fancy hotel room to do this?" Jillian's voice quivered. From sadness or anger, she couldn't be sure. *What about my news?*

"I thought we could have one last special night together—"

"So you put out the candles?"

"Look, okay fine. I thought, maybe after...you might need to blow off some steam. At the casinos or the spa or something."

Jillian said nothing. She'd been holding both champagne flutes in her right hand as part of her seductive pose, like a pair of delicate glass tulips. Now they felt heavy and the stems awkward between her fingers. She laid them on the bed between them. Then she started opening and closing her hands and fussing with her nails. The silence stretched until Calvin stood. He bent and gave her a platonic kiss on the cheek.

"We've had fun, Jilly." He crossed the room.

We've had fun, she thought. "'We've had fun?' Are you fucking kidding me, Cal? I love you!"

He continued toward the door. Jillian snatched one of the flutes off the bed and hurried after him. He must not have heard her because he didn't turn to face her. She crashed the glass over his head, leaving nothing but the base and a sharp stump of the stem in her trembling hand. Blood glistened in his dark hair, and several drops trickled onto the carpet. He turned, with a hand raised to his injury, and shot her a venomous look. Then he stormed from the room, slamming the door with such force that the other champagne flute rolled off the bed and shattered.

Three days had passed since that night in Atlantic City. Over and over, Jillian drove past Calvin's cozy, blue home, creeping down the street and straining for a glimpse of the world that existed behind the slightly parted drapes. She dropped off letters to him each day—sometimes a couple times a day—explaining how picture-perfect their lives could be together. Calvin made detective a couple of months earlier and could transfer anywhere. Jillian had just finished school and could be a psychologist anywhere. *Anywhere* remained a concept Jillian clung to because it meant their happiness. It meant starting a family of their own. Until then, she would keep driving past his snug, little house. She would keep dropping off letters. She didn't care that she left them at the home he shared with his wife. Jillian didn't care because her obsession left little room for caring.

Then her brazenness reached new heights: she dropped off a small package containing her worn, lacy panties.

That may have been the last straw for Calvin's wife. Jillian called later the same evening. The woman answered but didn't hand Calvin the phone as she'd done in the past. Her voice sounded sweet but firm. "Please don't call here anymore. Leave my husband alone, or you'll be sorry." Then she hung up. Maybe Calvin was right: his wife had had enough.

The woman had spoken softly, and Jillian thought she

heard Calvin's voice in the background shouting, "Who's on the phone, Suze?"

Finally a name. Probably short for Susan. But who was *Suze* to stand between them? He loved *Jillian.* She drove to their house, still determined not to let go of the first true love of her life. Not without a fight.

Parked across the street from the house, she called again. Susan answered. "Stop calling here, I mean it." She hung up. The lights were on in the house, but Jillian couldn't see inside.

She called again. And again. The phone rang. And rang. Each ring was more deafening than the one before as Jillian's rage escalated. She called Calvin's cell phone next; it went straight to voice mail. If only he would answer, she could blurt out her news and make him understand. All night, she called the house: no answer. She called his cell phone: voice mail. She reclined her seat and fell asleep.

The next day, late morning, Jillian awoke. Her cell phone had died. Calvin's car was gone, and she wondered if he'd even given her a second look as he drove down the street on his way to work. She opened the car door and unfolded herself from the confines of the car. Jillian headed across the street and rang the doorbell. She snickered as she approached. "Cozy little house..."

Calvin's wife answered with pressed lips. Jillian took in her appearance, seeing the woman clearly for the first time. Her alabaster skin, barely flushed at the cheeks, contrasted sharply with Jillian's maple-colored skin. Even the woman's hair was the exact opposite of Jillian's: pure golden sunshine that flowed well past her shoulders, encasing her in a gilded halo. Jillian wondered if the woman also noticed the differences, if she thought her husband just wanted something different. *Someone* different.

Jillian expected a defiant speech, but Susan invited Jillian in and offered her tea. Jillian sat and watched the waif-like woman glide out of the living room, curious to know if Susan always served as the hostess in her little stay-at-home world. Jillian squirmed in the cushioned chair while Calvin's wife tinkered away in the kitchen. She returned carrying a red, bone china tea set assembled neatly on a serving tray. The gold filigree matched the sunlight's glint off her hair.

The tea's warmth inside the delicate teacup radiated through to Jillian's fingertips. She found comfort in that and used it keep her voice steady and resolute. "I will not stop seeing Calvin."

The woman had made no efforts at introduction or other pleasantries other than offering tea. She sipped from her cup. "As I told you last night, you'll be sorry. I can't say it any plainer than that." Another sip.

Despite the steaming tea, the room felt cold, subzero even. Things felt wrong. Susan's words did not feel threatening; they felt like a warning. An oddly compassionate warning. Jillian's fingers itched to squirm beneath the saucer she held.

"If it weren't for our daughter, I'd gladly hand him over to you," the woman continued. "But Lyla would hate me if I divorced him. She idolizes him. She was crushed when I told her Calvin had cheated. She almost didn't believe me." She paused to sigh at the memory. "Regardless, I'm telling you, you'd end up about as happy as I am." Susan gestured to the whole of the room with her teacup before raising it to her lips. She lifted her eyes and peered over the teacup to catch Jillian's response. Met with neither words nor eye contact, she continued. "Oh, you thought you were the only one?" She stifled a snicker. "No, honey, not only are you *not* the only one Calvin's cheated on me with these past twenty-seven years, you're not even the only one right *now*."

Jillian's eyes stung with humiliation. Tears of burning, searing hatred built up and teetered, clinging desperately to her eyelashes. She failed to dam the waters. She cried. Not for the man who cared nothing for her dreams of being together anywhere in the country. For some reason, that fact had yet to register. When it did, she dismissed it. Instead, Jillian was infuriated by the fair-haired woman spouting off things that couldn't be true.

Calvin's wife rose from her seat. "More tea?"

Jillian still failed to find her words.

Susan shrugged, disappeared into the kitchen to put her cup and saucer away, and crossed back through the parlor before sulking up the stairs. "You can let yourself out," she called over her shoulder with a voice so drenched with melancholy, Jillian hoped she slipped on it and broke her neck.

Jillian sat still for an endless period of time. Then she stood, but not to let herself out. At first, she entered the kitchen to put away her teacup and saucer. Instead, she scanned the room. Next to a rotating wooden spice rack stood a knife block. The matte-red handles matched the crimson appliances and accents—and Jillian's own rage. The knives called to her, fanning the flames of her fury. Absentmindedly, she dumped the bone china items into her purse and grabbed the chef's knife from the block. Without even realizing where her footsteps fell, she went up the stairs after her lover's wife. The stairs creaked under her every step in protest, as if they knew how the early afternoon would unfold.

But how could they? Jillian didn't even know what would happen next. She didn't know she would lunge at the woman at the end of the hallway. Didn't know the hardwood floor beneath the carpeted runner would croak, warning Susan of her movements. Jillian also didn't know one of Susan's pastimes included kick-boxing cardio classes with her daughter at the gym on Saturday mornings.

Calvin's wife ducked at the noise and spun around with surprising precision.

Still, Jillian's body kept up the assault without the consent of her mind. A bony fist flew into Jillian's jaw; her teeth pinched off the tip of her tongue. She realized then she'd only been struck because one of her arms instinctively protected her abdomen.

The two women tumbled into the bedroom, caught in a knot of arms and legs, thrashing and screeching and grunting. Still clutching the kitchen knife, Jillian lashed out as soon as she found ample room for her arm to arc.

Susan blocked with her right forearm and immediately cried out. The blade had caught near her wrist and slid through her flesh easily, parting her skin all the way up to the inside of her elbow. The blow brought her to the floor.

Blood painted the world red. The walls. The floors. Them. Their journey was punctuated in splatters and smears. A stunned Jillian, still tasting her own blood, backed up. Susan slumped down, propped up against the bed, bleeding steadily at Jillian's feet.

Badly injured, but not out of the fight yet, Calvin's wife staggered to her feet. At that moment, Jillian snapped to the present just long enough to admire the woman's spirit. Susan looked at her wound, and instead of pressing it to staunch the bleeding, she stared intently at the dribbling flow of red for a second. Her shoulders went slack, her defiant spirit broken. Jillian thought Susan may have conceded her fate, resigned to die.

They stood for a single, fleeting second, glaring into each other's eyes. Susan's were a mottled blue, like a roiling, storm-strewn sea, Jillian's a glittering, bright chestnut. Then Susan crumpled and her already fair skin faded to white. The fight Jillian had admired in her eyes faded as well. Life left her.

Jillian left soon after.

Jillian retreated to her apartment and sat on the floor. She backed into the darkest shadow with her knees pulled to her chest. Covered in the blood of her lover's wife, Jillian was all alone to process what she'd done.

Days passed beyond the windows of her room. Eating never entered Jillian's mind, and her lips crackled from dehydration. The carpet beneath her grew damp and foul with waste. Jillian's mind fell quiet and empty, overcome by shock. She thought of nothing except for the blood. She would never forget the blood. She could still taste it.

The intercom by the apartment door buzzed. *How many days had passed?* Static and distance prevented Jillian from making out the voice, or its words, from her bedroom. Certain her visitor wasn't anyone concerned with her well-being, she ignored whoever rang the doorbell. She forced herself to unfold from the fetal ball she'd formed in the corner. In a trance, she peeled her stiff clothes from her body. Blood had soaked through to her skin and thoroughly dried, leaving deep crimson lines from the folds of the fabric, and giving her coffee-colored skin the appearance of a tattered map.

Jillian sat on the floor of the shower, mesmerized by the water swirling around the drain. The steam only slightly defeated the cold of the ceramic surface beneath her. Hot water hit the crown of her head, plastering her thick hair to her shoulders. She had killed someone. An innocent woman. Someone's daughter. Possibly someone's sister. Lyla's mother. Calvin's wife. She'd killed Calvin's wife. Her name was *Susannah*, not Susan, as she'd originally presumed. Jillian had learned her name from Channel 6 news. She'd left her TV on when she rushed to Calvin's house and hadn't had the presence of mind to turn it off when she returned. Only one other piece of information had managed to get through the haze and fog of the last seventy-two hours: the police were calling Susannah's death a suicide. That was good news for Jillian. Apparently, pocketing the teacup proved practical. So she asked herself, *Why don't I feel relieved?*

Jillian exited the shower, dressed, and plugged in her phone to call her family and close friends. Then she laughed hysterically. She had none of either. Longing for someone she could assure of her well-being—though she most decidedly was not well—she dialed Mel's number. Mel had moved back to Ohio right after graduation, about a month after the mugging. So entrenched was Jillian in her relationship with Calvin that she'd barely lifted her head to say goodbye. Jillian regretted that. They could hardly be considered close friends, but they had bonded enough after the mugging that Mel had practically become the only friend Jillian had.

"Where the hell have you been?" Mel screeched. Jillian still hadn't eaten and her head throbbed with its own pulse, palpitating in her ears. She held the phone a foot from her face, but she could still hear her former roommate clearly. "I've been calling you. Your phone just kept going to voice mail. I didn't know what happened to you in that fucking city."

"Relax, Mel." The irony was not lost on Jillian that she had contributed to the city's swelling crime rate, even if Susannah's death had technically been ruled a suicide. "I'm fine."

"What happened?"

"Nothing." Although her phone was nowhere near fully charged, Jillian unplugged it, allowing her to pace throughout the apartment.

"Don't tell me nothing."

"It's...Cal."

Mel sighed. "You're still seeing that piece of shit married cop? Really, Jill, you can do so much better." Mel had found out about Calvin when he showed up at graduation, and she never held back her disapproval of the relationship.

"Spare me right now, okay? It's something else. I don't want to talk about it over the phone."

"Oh my God, he knocked you up. You didn't tell him, did you? Don't tell him. You've seen those Lifetime movies, right? Dudes get crazy when their mistresses get pregnant." Mel placed an awkward emphasis on the word "mistresses" as if it were foreign to her vernacular.

Jillian chuckled nervously. "I'm not pregnant, Mel."

"Well, what is it then?"

"Nothing. Never mind. I shouldn't have called you. I gotta go." Jillian listened to Mel's garbled voice for a few more seconds before hanging up and reconnecting her cell phone to its charger. She'd thought she craved human contact, but her rapid breathing and blurry tears proved she wasn't ready yet.

The next day, Jillian's bedroom door swung open. Mel ambled in carrying several bags of groceries and clutching a bottle of vodka by its neck. Jillian would have preferred something she could actually drink, but she should have expected nothing less from Mel.

"Still have your keys, I see," Jillian said. Despite the late afternoon hour, she remained buried under the covers. Their weight bore down on her like a physical manifestation of her guilt. She kicked at them and, once free, sat up against her pillows. "What'd you do—drive all night after we hung up?"

"Of course not. I flew out this morning. And *we* did not hang up. *You* hung up. *I* was still talking. I don't know what the fuck's wrong with you, but I felt like it might be serious." Mel searched the room, and her gaze fell to the dark stain in the corner. A scrub brush and a canister of foaming carpet cleaner lay near it. Neither had done much for the stain. Mel wrinkled her nose. "Looks like I was right. Besides, I needed to ship the rest of my stuff out to Ohio. I see you boxed it up for me. You should move them away from the door though. I almost tripped and broke my face."

"You're welcome."

"Yeah, yeah. Get up. Outta bed."

Jillian followed Mel to the living room and told her everything about her affair with Calvin, her subsequent mindless obsession with him, and confronting Susannah. Killing her. Jillian shuddered when she heard the words spoken aloud.

Shocked by Jillian's story, Mel practically poured the vodka down her throat and cursed herself for only bringing one bottle. When Mel wasn't drinking, she sat on her hands to keep them from trembling. Jillian had only seen her do that once before: the night of the mugging. She started to question whether she'd confided in the right person.

Finally, Jillian said, "I think I should turn myself in."

"I think those are the dumbest words you've ever uttered," Mel said before whipping her head back to swallow another shot. The glass clinked against her new lip piercing. When she snapped upright again, she brushed her angled bangs out of her eyes. Her hair was dyed pink.

"I'm serious. I can't live with this...this feeling."

"I thought you said you saw the news? That's how you learned her name, right? Didn't you also *learn* that the lady committed suicide? You're off the hook. Now drink up." Mel poured herself another shot and knocked it back.

Jillian swirled her vodka and orange juice. She could never drink liquor straight like Mel, especially now. She took tiny sips of the screwdriver, but she only allowed the drink to touch her lips. If any entered her mouth, she discreetly released it back into the cup. They sat in silence for a long while. Well, Jillian was silent. Mel chattered on about the aches of moving back home and how cute her philosophy professor would be if he dyed his hair black and dressed "darker."

Jillian nodded and pretended to be grateful for the distraction. A few hours passed before she ushered her friend out. When they reached the door, she grabbed Mel's arm. "If anything happens to me—if anything ever happens to me— the bloody clothes, the knife, the teacup I stole, everything is in a shoe box in my closet. No matter what, there will always be a shoe box."

Mel yanked her arm free. "Jill, you're freaking me out. What do you mean 'if anything happens to you'?"

"Just promise, okay? Two days from now, twenty years

from now...You're the only one who knows the truth. One day, I want Calvin's daughter to know the truth, too. About her mother. It's the least I can do." Jillian paused and swallowed hard. She preferred her fidgety hands over her urge to caress her belly. "If it were me, I'd want my child to know the truth. So promise." Jillian nodded emphatically, waiting for her former roommate to agree.

"All right, all right, I fucking promise," Mel said, visibly shaken. She loitered in the doorway as though she wanted to say or do more. "I'll call you later. But I still think you should burn that shoe box."

3

Home is Where Your Story Begins.

LYLA CRADLED HER mother's lifeless body. Her essence had leaked from the lengthy, jagged cut in her forearm. Blood had crept through her blue shirt like a plague, turning it purple with infection. Lyla Kyle felt her own life ending. She may have been daddy's little girl, but she confided in her mother, her best friend. Lyla lowered her mother back to the bedroom floor and brushed her fingers over her mother's vacant eyes. If Lyla ignored the blood, she could almost imagine her mother had fallen asleep on the floor.

Lyla should have seen it coming: her father's infidelity, her mother's withdrawn demeanor increasing every day. The night before, she'd visited for dinner and the phone rang. She could tell by her mother's austere tone that it was one of her father's girlfriends. When her mom returned to the table, the atmosphere cooled and conversation lulled to a standstill. Lyla had practically scratched her way out of the house after dinner. If only she'd stayed.

Then realization clouded her features: her father had caused her mother's death. His lies, his cheating—her mother couldn't take it anymore. Lyla had just found her own apartment, essentially leaving her mother alone. How could her father have been so blind? How could he not see how his actions affected her? Lyla stood and crossed the room. Her sanity cracked and shattered like the glass exploding around her as she punched the mirror above her parents' bureau. Each sliver reflected her mother's corpse as it spiraled through the air—a million reminders magnifying Lyla's grief.

The front door opened. Lyla had left it unlocked when she'd called the police. She heard footsteps on the stairs, and voices.

"Did someone call my brother?" a familiar female voice asked.

"He's on his way, ma'am," a man, presumably a detective, replied.

"Did dispatch tell her not to touch anything?" a different man asked.

Then the female voice again. "You expect her not to touch her dead mother?"

"This is why you shouldn't be here, LeeAnn. You're too close to this. It sounds like a cut-and-dry suicide. Our office shouldn't even be here."

"But I appreciate you making an exception for my family, boss."

Lyla heard it all. She wept and stared at the empty space where the mirror had been, trying to avoid the scene behind her. Fewer footsteps made their way down the hallway, growing ever closer until they entered the bedroom. Without turning, Lyla knew who the woman was: her aunt LeeAnn, Associate Medical Examiner.

LeeAnn placed a tender hand on Lyla's shoulder. "Sweetie, you should come with me. We have to get you out of those clothes."

"What?" Lyla glared at her aunt, stunned by her sterile nature. It matched her appearance: pallid cheeks framed by chin-length dark hair that had lost its luster years ago. She worked with death, and it showed.

"You might have evidence on your person. We have to take your clothes and give them to the technicians to bag and label." She met Lyla's glare before continuing. "I know this is difficult for you. I'm sorry."

"'Difficult for me?' My mother just killed herself because she couldn't spend another day with *your* brother!"

LeeAnn cleared her throat. Lyla watched her aunt's eyes awkwardly shift sideways behind the narrow lenses of her glasses. "You don't know for sure that's what happened, dear," LeeAnn said in a hushed tone. Clearly, Lyla had embarrassed her in front of the numerous technicians and police personnel mulling about the house.

"Don't 'dear' me. You saw her in there. She slit her wrist to the elbow!"

"I understand you're upset, but her death has to be treated as a homicide and then *ruled* a suicide. That's how this works."

"Can you do me a favor and stop being a medical examiner for two seconds and be an aunt? Please?" Lyla's voice quivered.

Despite her petite size, LeeAnn quieted and guided her niece without effort, around the body and out of the room. Lyla felt her aunt's fingers, cold underneath the latex gloves, caressing her hand as they stumbled through the blood-soaked hall. Lyla wondered if she'd ever forget that sharp, metallic smell.

As they descended the stairs, Lyla realized her aunt was the worst possible person to comfort her through a tragedy. She was so callous and calculating. Then she saw him—her father—rushing through the living room. He moved in to hug her, and she almost retched.

Lyla shouldered past her father, leaving him gaping with confusion. Thankfully, LeeAnn kept him from chasing her. Lyla stormed down to the basement laundry room, hoping to find something to change into so she could hand her current clothing over to her anxious aunt. The thought of going back up to the bedroom to borrow something from her mother muddled Lyla's consciousness, causing both her vision and her stomach to stir.

Nothing was on the folding table, but when Lyla opened the dryer, she found a full load of clothes and rifled through them. She set aside her father's shirts as she imagined her mother washing lipstick stains and women's perfume from them for who knew how many years. Lyla found a pair of workout pants and her mom's favorite T-shirt: the faded, primrose-yellow one she wore when she painted or tended her herb garden. Lyla clutched the soft cotton to her face. Even fresh out of the dryer, it still smelled like her. Lyla shed a single tear into it before putting it aside and removing her clothes.

"Ms. Kyle?" an unfamiliar voice called from the top of the stairs—probably one of the technicians.

Then her aunt said, "Lyla, are you decent?"

"I'm getting something to wear," Lyla huffed.

"Okay, I'm just going to bring down this bag"—she started down the stairs—"and then I'll give you a minute of privacy."

A whole minute. Lyla took the bag without objection but avoided looking her aunt in the eyes. LeeAnn's obsession with the *evidence* agitated Lyla. Clearly, her mother killed herself. It *was* clear, wasn't it?

As Lyla rolled her blood-dampened shirt over her head, the collar snagged on the back of her earring and sent it flying across the laundry room. Lyla followed it, hunching to avoid hitting her head on the low-hanging ceiling beams. As she approached the tiny silver stud, she heard muffled voices above her in the living room.

"She thinks *I* did this?"

Her father. Hearing his voice, Lyla felt a heavy coiling in her gut, like thick, knotted rope.

"I didn't say that. She thinks you caused this." They remained silent for a moment, then LeeAnn continued. "I'm not so sure it's a suicide, Calvin."

Lyla stumbled backward, aghast. She managed to take a breath and perk her ears in the direction of the ceiling.

"What makes you say that?" her father asked.

"Well, for one, I can't find the knife Susannah used on herself. And there were no hesitation marks anywhere on her arm. I think it's highly unlikely that someone as—how should I say this—*docile* as Susannah would just commit to and inflict an eight-inch gash to herself without second thoughts."

What Lyla heard next caused fire to rise to her cheeks.

"Did Lyla and Susannah get along well? Maybe they'd argued recently?"

"So let me get this straight. My daughter thinks *I* did it, and you think *she* did it? What is going on? I can't deal with this right now."

"You're a cop; you know how this works. Your men and my office will investigate this as a homicide until everyone can conclusively rule otherwise. I'm sorry I'm asking the hard questions you don't want to hear, but it's not like you won't be asked them again during the course of the investigation." She paused and, in a quieter tone Lyla could barely decipher, continued. "I want to see justice done for all involved. But I'm not so sure my boss does. He retires in two weeks, and ultimately, it's his call. If he smells suicide, that's the box he'll check on the death certificate."

Lyla heard her father grunt in protest, but from the sound of the creaking floorboards, they parted ways. Her father's heavier footsteps became fainter as LeeAnn's softer footfalls grew louder, heading Lyla's way. Lyla stuffed her clothes and sneakers into the evidence bag and took the steps two at a time, beating LeeAnn to the doorway. She threw the bag of clothes in her aunt's face and ran barefoot to her car without a word.

Faded blue scrubs and starched white lab coats buzzed around Lyla. Their steady flow was parted only by a tented yellow sign that read Caution Wet Floor. The men and women streamed around it seamlessly as though it were a boulder in a river. The difference between Lyla and her colleagues was that they had somewhere to go.

Lyla shuffled, bewildered, through the halls of West Philadelphia General Hospital. She shouldn't be there. She'd been granted leave due to her mother's passing, yet Lyla couldn't stay away. She needed to be there, needed to be in the hospital where her mother had given her life. *But why?* Did she think that was where she would figure out what to do with that life? Maybe she just needed a sign. And not the Caution Wet Floor sign.

Lyla glanced back at the scuffed yellow sign, and when she faced front again, a friendly face stood in her path. He pushed a pharmaceutical cart, and if he hadn't looked up from his phone at that moment, he would have bulldozed into her.

"Lyla, what are you doing here? I heard what happened.

39

I'm so sorry about your mom." He placed his free hand on her shoulder, caressing her with his thumb. "I tried to call..."

CJ and Lyla had shared classes as undergrads. He had taken a position as a pharmacist at the same time Lyla began her first year of residency. Working alongside each other had made them close, although Lyla suspected he longed to become even closer.

His normally skittish demeanor seemed intensified, as though he were in a rush. A thin layer of perspiration glistened in the valleys between the acne peppering his face. Lyla presumed he was juggling tasks.

"I know. Thank you, CJ." Lyla placed her hand on top of his, rubbed it briefly, and coaxed it off of her shoulder. She held his hand just long enough to disguise the act of removing it. "I just can't sit home right now."

"Yeah, but you wouldn't be alone. You'd be with your family."

Lyla wanted to say something like *Fuck family*, but she decided against it. "I know this sounds weird, but I just want to act like everything's normal, at least until I'm ready to deal with the fact that it's not."

"Well, in that case"—CJ cleared his throat—"excuse me, Dr. Kyle, can you bring this to Dr. Chambers in the O.R.? I gotta get back to my station."

He shoved a hard plastic tray toward her. The compartments' contents were sealed in with a translucent, peel-away film.

"Now you wouldn't be trying to get me in trouble, would you, CJ?" Lyla asked with her head tilted playfully, batting her lashes. Everyone knew non-pharmacy personnel weren't supposed to handle controlled supplies unless they were the prescribing physician.

"Of course not. Actually, just walk with me. Is Dr. Chambers' O.R. on the way to...Where did you say you were headed?"

Lyla eyed the tray. A fresh one was brought to each O.R. prior to surgery, and unused vials and materials were returned to the pharmacy and inventoried. The patient was billed for the items that were used. Lyla thought about the tray's contents: multiple vials of medications intended to quell different surgical emergencies. One drug stood out. One could be as fatal as it was helpful: succinylcholine.

Anectine, its commercial name, was used to help intubate a patient under anesthesia. It relaxed muscles, even the ones that facilitated breathing. Since the patient was on a ventilator, that wasn't a problem. *But if one wasn't on a ventilator...*

"Lyla?"

"Yes, of course. I'm sorry. I don't even know what I'm doing here. I'm not headed anywhere. I can take a walk."

Lyla strolled beside CJ but contributed little to the conversation. She felt a plan forming. She wondered if revenge was one of the five steps of the grieving process, but that thought was quickly dispelled by the memory of something even more magical about succinylcholine: it was virtually imperceptible in a dead body. It metabolized too fast, and whatever components it left behind were already present in the human body. Elevated levels could be expertly argued away in a court of law. She recalled the Coppolino case of 1966 where the jury acquitted the infamous doctor of murder. Sure, he was convicted of a second murder, but Lyla chose to focus on the positive. She tried to keep her face solemn, but she still grinned like a fool, which served her well: CJ had apparently just made a joke.

Lyla needed to get a hold of the drug. It was perfect, the sign she'd hoped for. But how could she obtain it? Unused vials were brought right back to the pharmacy. Lyla's forehead furrowed and her grin dissolved into a frown as she puzzled over her newfound purpose and the obstacle it presented.

Lyla and CJ neared the operating room where Dr. Chambers would soon perform laparoscopic surgery. She smiled briefly at those prepping the room before remembering that she was supposed to be grieving, not giddy with the idea of exacting revenge on her father.

CJ knocked on the outer door, and an anesthesia tech emerged from the inner O.R., already donning her sterilized paper accessories. She received the tray and returned to the inner room. Through the window, Lyla watched the tech peel the film back and slide the tray into an empty slot in the anesthesia cart. On Lyla's way back out to the hallway—CJ was already there, gazing at her—she nodded at the nurses. Then a collection of boxes in the corner caught her attention.

The receptacle that had caught her attention was similar to the biohazardous waste and sharps receptacles next to it. Doctors used it to discard vials of drugs used during surgery—even those not entirely empty. The vials' occlusive rubber stoppers kept the unused portions from leaking out and sloshing around in the box. 10ccs of succinylcholine was a lethal dose. A few leftover vials would be more than sufficient. *How often is that box cleared out?*

With her head down, she joined CJ. His gaze had morphed from longing to quizzical, either because of the length of time she'd lingered or because Lyla had realized she wasn't ready to return to work and it showed on her face. Not just yet, she thought, but not due to conventional reasons. She didn't need to *grieve* the loss of her mother, but rather *avenge* the loss of her mother.

CJ placed a sweaty hand on the small of Lyla's back. She felt the moisture through her scrubs and her mother's favorite yellow shirt, which she was wearing under her scrubs.

"So, you said you weren't scheduled anywhere?" he asked.

"Yeah. Actually, I think I'm gonna see if I can get out of here. Take that leave they offered, even if only a day or two. I'm not ready to be back. I thought I was, but...Plus, I want to gather some things of my mom's and bring them to my new apartment," she lied. "Do you think they have empty cardboard boxes in the supply room?"

Lyla hoped that sounded like a plausible reason to visit the supply room. She *did* need a box she could conceal the receptacle in, but she could swipe some empty syringes there as well.

"They should. Do you need help? I get off in a few hours." CJ looked at his watch.

"No, thanks. Anthony's gonna meet me at my parents' house." Another lie.

"I didn't think you two were still...I mean...I'm sorry, I just haven't heard you speak of him in a while."

"It's been rocky, but he's been pretty supportive since..."

"Well that's good. I'm glad someone's there for you."

Lyla's phone rang. She tugged it from her pocket and scanned the caller I.D. It was Anthony. She held the phone up and shrugged at CJ. "Speak of the devil, huh?"

CJ frowned even though Lyla let the call go to voice mail. They parted ways, and when Lyla passed another operating room, she peeked in to gauge the size of the box. Perhaps she'd return later under the guise of retrieving more cardboard boxes. The hospital would be emptier, especially the operating rooms. Proud of her plan's infant stages, Lyla called Anthony back and let him know she was, in fact, working—and working late.

The day of Lyla's mother's funeral, it rained. Not a heavy rain, but a fine mist that encompassed the mourners in added sadness. Though Lyla sat wedged between her aunt and her father, her mind couldn't have been further from the diminutive woman to her left, the aunt who suspected Lyla of killing her own mother. Nor could her heart have been further from the man to her right, the father whom Lyla suspected was the catalyst of her mother's suicide. The three of them sat stoically at the front of the rows of attendees, tear ducts barren, their usually olive skin pale against their dark hair and attire.

At the conclusion of the services, Lyla rose to her feet. If she stared at her mother's coffin any longer, she'd be tempted to jump in the grave beside it. When LeeAnn and her father approached her parents' next-door neighbors, Lyla joined them.

"I'm gonna head home," Lyla said, addressing neither of them in particular. She'd already made up her mind to skip the repast altogether. Besides, she had plans for that evening.

Her aunt's eyes widened in alarm. "You're not going to join us at your parents' house for lunch?"

"It's not my 'parents' house' anymore. It's just *his* house now, isn't it?" Lyla indicated her father with a shift of her gaze.

Calvin said, "I think your mother would have wanted you to celebrate her life with family and friends, Lyla."

"What do *you* know about what Mom wanted?"

Her words stung them both, but neither retorted, so Lyla spun on her heels and left, drifting through the crowd and misty rain. The damp, spongy earth made a sucking noise with each footstep, and she almost didn't hear her phone vibrating against her keys in her pocket. She answered without looking.

"Why didn't you tell me your mother's *funeral* was *today*?" Anthony bellowed.

Lyla was startled by his volume. "I wasn't sure if I wanted you there, and I didn't know how to tell you that." Her boyfriend kept shouting, so Lyla continued sarcastically. "I'm doing fine after just burying my mother, though. Thanks for asking."

"I'm sorry, you're right. I just wish you would've told me. I wanted to be there for you. I've asked you over and over when and where the services were being held."

He paused, and Lyla didn't know what to say. He was right. But after seeing what her father had driven her mother to, something about having a significant other by her side made Lyla's stomach sour.

"Can I pick you up?" he asked, finally ending the silence.

"No." Realizing she'd responded too curtly, Lyla sighed. "I have...plans. I mean, I just want to be alone tonight. Please try to understand. I don't know how to deal with this, but I do know I wannna deal with it alone."

"Okay, but if you change your mind, which I hope you do, please call me."

Lyla agreed and hung up. She wished she hadn't mentioned having plans. Hopefully, Anthony wouldn't dwell on her tiny slip-up later on.

Lyla reached her apartment and readied herself for the

evening, laying several items out on her bed. The days between her mother's death and burial had allowed Lyla's need for revenge to fester in her heart and mind. She'd suffered many emotions during the past few days, but revenge was the only one remaining, the only thing that mattered. Her father was responsible, that much was clear. She had to make him pay. She had to get justice for her mother. She had to make things right.

That night, her father would take his last breath.

Lyla waited while the clouds marched in from the horizon, thickening with every mile and blackening Philadelphia with gloom. The somber mist that had engulfed the day was followed by a deluge of heavy rain and thundering fury that night. When the sky opened up, the late summer humidity dissipated, but Lyla's anger towards her father hadn't cooled.

She stared at the items she'd laid out on her couch. Her gaze lingered on the receptacle she'd stolen from the hospital the other night. Lyla had needed to break its lock open to retrieve the vials inside. Shards of hard plastic still lay scattered on her living room floor. Lyla stepped over them, snatched several vials of her chosen drug and a syringe, and tossed them in her bag. Then she grabbed the liter of Jack Daniel's whiskey—her father's preferred brand—and the lighter.

Lyla eased her car to a stop a few blocks away from *his* house. A low-hanging branch scraped the roof. Lyla cringed at the sound, almost as if it were begging Lyla to return her foot to the gas pedal. But she did not. She parked, drew 10 ccs of succinylcholine into the syringe, and slithered out of the car into the wet night. She hurried to her destination in a half-crouch, trying to blend into the darkness of the asphalt.

She sneaked around the back of her father's house through the shadows of the maple trees. They still clutched their leaves in denial of the approaching autumn. Every now and again, the rain would tear a leaf from its branch and the fluttering shadow would frighten Lyla. But instead of cursing the rain, she thanked it. It softened the ground, cushioned her footfalls, and tethered the neighbors to their couches. Few, if any, people would witness her arrival.

Searching for signs of life in *his* house and finding only the soft flickering of a TV in the living room, Lyla entered through the back door. Despite burying his wife hours earlier, her father had gone on a date that night. She'd overheard him bragging about it to a group of his colleagues at the funeral. A few were impressed by his gall, but most were repulsed.

However loathsome Lyla found it, she'd learned from her mother that, following a date night, her father would drunkenly pass out on the couch, which was good for Lyla, logistically. She imagined his stench: sex and a perfume so cheap the woman probably purchased it at the cosmetics counter of the nearest drug store. For a second, she marveled at how he at least had the decency not to bring the girls to the house where his wife—her mother, for God's sake—had lost her life.

She knew the bristles of the doormat made a *scritch-scritch* noise, so Lyla bent each leg and thoroughly and silently dried the soles of her sneakers on her pants' legs. Without squeaking, wet shoes, she tiptoed down to the basement, pausing to grab a candle from the emergency kit at the top of the stairs. The old house's circuit breakers were notoriously fickle, so she switched off the main breaker, drowning the house in complete darkness. Lyla paused in the spot where she'd overheard her aunt's suspicions only days earlier. With her ear toward the ceiling, she strained to hear any indication of her father's stirring over the din of rain pelting the house. She heard nothing, so she removed the hypodermic needle from her over-sized bag, almost piercing herself as she fumbled for it.

"*Here I come, Daddy,*" she said in a singsong whisper, creeping back up the stairs.

Lyla found her father prone on the couch, three quarters of his face buried in a pillow dampened by his own sweat and drool. Before she'd hit the circuit breaker, the TV had probably been playing a rerun of *Law & Order*. An empty whiskey bottle stood on the coffee table. She imagined her father being too drunk to notice it obstructing the television, partially distorting the image through the curvature of the glass. Lyla squatted between the sofa and the table, holding the needle firmly. She punched the tip into the sluggish pulsing of his jugular vein and plunged the chemical into his bloodstream. He didn't budge, and he never would again. Calvin Kyle didn't deserve such an easy ending.

In the following minutes, Lyla toured the house. The carpet runner that once lined the upstairs hallway had been removed, revealing dull, unfinished hardwood. Exposed staples tugged at her shoe soles. Fresh paint fumes tickled her nose. None of it fooled Lyla. She still saw the blood. She still wrestled against tears as the copper odor assaulted her with every breath.

Lyla faced the difficulty in being there head on as she scuttled around grabbing whatever items she wished to salvage. She knew she needed to be there to move forward, and she intended to take her mother with her. She grabbed her mother's blown-glass oil lamps from the master bedroom nightstands, a gift from LeeAnn that Lyla had coveted for years. She stopped to admire the painting above the headboard. It depicted the Philadelphia Art Museum from the riverbank, drenched in the orange glow of sunset. The canvas was three feet by two feet, and Lyla and her mother had worked on it in tandem, using a postcard as their inspiration. Lyla wished she could take it with her, but it was too cumbersome—and would be too suspicious.

Lyla tiptoed around the blood stain that had soaked into the floorboards and found her mother's tortoise shell reading glasses and matching case in the bathroom. Her mother hardly used them, but sometimes she wore them perched on her head to hold her bangs back or she would chew on the temple tip when she read. Lyla sniffled at the image and jogged back downstairs to snatch her mother's bone china tea set from the dining room cabinet. Lyla found only three teacups, but without time to search for the fourth, she cushioned the remaining pieces of the set with the old T-shirts she'd brought. The trinkets clamored against each other in her bag as she returned to the living room.

Lyla took nothing of her father's.

Standing over the couch, she withdrew the plain white, tapered candle from her bag and lit it with the metallic Zippo lighter her mother had given her when Lyla graduated pre-med. The engraving on the lighter read HOME IS WHERE YOUR STORY BEGINS. *Ironic*, she scoffed, since her story had just begun. Her mother. Then her father. Death was Lyla's story. With that thought, she held the lit candle near the magazines on the coffee table. The paper ignited slowly at first, the flames only gently caressing the surface of the pages. She blew on them gently to coax the fledgling fire to swell.

Satisfied with the lit magazines, Lyla pulled the whiskey from her bag. The cap crackled when she twisted it open. She sloshed it all over the couch and her father. One of her mother's oil lamps tumbled out of her shoulder bag and smashed against the edge of the table. The flames dancing among the magazines ignited the lamp oil. Lyla stepped back as the fire spread from the table to the carpet and beyond. It crawled up the sides of the couch with red and orange fingers, clawing at her father. The flames licked the drapes and formed a fiery tent above her. Just as a boom of thunder shook the old house, Lyla backed out of the room where the fire raged and consumed her father's body. She exited the way she came, never looked back, and tried to forget that she was ever daddy's little girl.

Outside, embers flitted and flurried around her. Safe from the blossoming inferno, Lyla lingered in the back yard for a few moments to bask in the heat of her childhood home. It burned despite the rain. Almost in defiance of it. Something about the burning home beckoned her like a setting summer sun on the horizon. When the flames took over, triumphant in their fiery invasion, Lyla sprinted into the street, a mask of panic plastered on her face, along with her wet hair.

"Help! My father! Someone help!" she screamed, fighting to be heard against the roar of the storm. The neighbors emerged from their homes, some to help, some to gape. One of the next-door neighbors—the same one from the funeral—approached Lyla.

"I called 911," he said. "The fire department's on its way. Lyla, are you all right?"

Lyla heard the neighbor perfectly, but she stared at him with wild eyes, pretending to be too distraught to understand him. He clasped her hand and led her farther across the street, presumably to distance them from the house in case it exploded. Before long, they heard the sirens in the distance. A sedan pulled up and screeched to a stop, beating the fire trucks to the scene. In the flickering light of the burning home, Lyla saw a large, rigid antenna standing out from the back of the sedan's roof. A barrier separated the front seat from the back. It was an unmarked police car.

A man with boyish features, betrayed only by the creases around his eyes, jumped out and grabbed her shoulders. "Is anyone inside?" He shook her and demanded again, "Is anyone inside? Is your father in there?"

Lyla didn't have to feign confusion anymore. The stranger's mention of her father had genuinely taken her aback. *Does he know me?* She thought of the car he'd pulled up in; he probably worked with her father. He may even have attended her mother's funeral. She wondered if he'd heard about her father's date.

"He's unconscious," she sobbed. Through her tears, mustered by thoughts of vengeance for her mother, she managed to add, "I couldn't move him."

Lyla felt a jab of guilt when the man sped toward the house. He shouldn't have gone in. He should have waited for the fire department.

He never came out.

4
Next of Kin.

WHEN JASON BRIGHTHOUSE Jr. crossed through the doorway, home early from class, something seemed off. The air felt wrong. Two police officers stood in the foyer, blocking his view of his mother, but he heard her wailing. Instinctively, he welled up, too, that familiar stinging sensation prickling his face. She peered past the officers at him, her bronze hair frizzed and her jade eyes rimmed with red. Her eyes told Jason his father was dead.

The cops tried to console them. "You both should know that he died valiantly while trying to save a fellow officer from his burning home," one of them said.

Their words sounded far away. Only his mother's sobs were up close and personal. She and Jason had spent their whole lives trying to prepare themselves for that moment while praying it would never come. Being a police officer came with risks, especially in Philadelphia. But they had expected bullets, not back drafts.

The two officers poured out more information. Words tumbled from their mouths and spilled down the fronts of their cheap suits. Cheap suits. Like the ones his father wore. The men were fellow detectives. Jason should have known the department wouldn't send mere beat officers to notify the next of kin of one of their own. Jason teared up at the thought of him and his mother being reduced to 'next of kin.' Instead, he tried to focus on the men's words, which were doing so little to quell his tears. He tugged his fingers through his thick, curly hair, eventually settling his head in his hands. As he listened, sniffling, eyes closed, he learned that his father knew the other man, another detective.

"We think Detective Brighthouse heard the call over the scanner and recognized the address. Though he was off duty, he'd been driving around in the vicinity of the residence and rushed to save his colleague."

Jason felt as if the words were coming from another household, happening to another family.

But the second officer continued. "The detective he attempted to save had a wife and daughter. Unfortunately, his wife committed suicide earlier this week. Perhaps he didn't want the family to be struck with two tragic losses in one week."

But why didn't he think of his own family? Jason returned to that question over and over. He wished he could be strong, proud of his father's selfless act, but Jason stubbornly refused to chase away his selfish thoughts.

Before Jason and his mother fell asleep on the couch, neither wanting to retreat to their own rooms, his mother spoke. As far as he could remember, it was the first time she'd done so that day. She said, "He must have thought if it were him in a burning house, he'd want someone to help him return home to us."

Those words touched Jason. He knew they were true. He knew she echoed his father's sentiments exactly.

Three days later, Jason and his mother sat huddled together against the chilly air. The motorcade for the dual funeral for Brighthouse Sr. and his colleague was tremendous, snaking through the city for blocks, but nothing compared to the actual turnout. Hundreds of men and women came to pay their respects to the two fallen detectives.

Jason recognized some of the uniformed officers from the Police Athletic League and family barbecues. Strips of black cloth cut across each of their badges. A sea of solemn faces swayed to the bagpiper's rendition of "Amazing Grace". With everyone so lost in their collective grief, hardly a body remained still when the rifle squad shot three volleys into the air. The resounding crash rattled Jason's chest, but he sat motionless, among the few who didn't flinch.

Desperate for something to focus on besides his own grief, Jason watched the honor guard split to fold two separate flags. They placed one in his mother's trembling hands. They brought the other to a young woman across the aisle. She acted oddly disinterested in the ritual, all but tossing the flag onto the chair beside her. Jason recalled the detectives' mention of the daughter who had lost her mother and father to isolated incidents in the same week. Judging by her front-row seat, that was her. Her demeanor confused Jason; her body wasn't heaving with sobs, nor was she clutching any used tissues. *Strange for a daughter who'd lost both her parents.* Up until then, he'd empathized with her; he wasn't so sure anymore.

She sat alone, empty seats flanking her on both sides. A man around her age sat directly behind her and rubbed her shoulders, but she continued to stoically observe the services as though he didn't exist. The sheer black scarf around her head fluttered in the breeze, and the large, dark sunglasses either shielded her from prying stares or served to hide her emotionless eyes. Jason feared it was the latter. Something about her utter stillness and defiant posture troubled him.

Beneath the scarf, her hair was as black as the damp soil

of the freshly dug graves. She resembled a picture of Jackie O. he had seen once. Maybe that's how she sneaked through Jason's grief and grabbed his attention while so many others had gone unnoticed. When her father's casket disappeared from view into the fresh grave, she stood to toss in a single rose. Jason watched her movements and studied her face. The other mourners repeatedly lifted tissues to their eyes and noses, lifting their sunglasses if necessary. Not her. Her features were fresh and young, but she appeared worn, as though the compounding tragedies had aged her. *Then why wasn't she crying?*

While ushers lowered the casket of the woman's father into the plot beside her mother's, another group of men transported Jason's father's casket to a separate part of the cemetery. The crowd split, and Jason noticed another young woman. She approached from the road, watching her footsteps. *Is she just now arriving?*

She stood alone, and he watched her as he had the other woman. She clung to the outskirts of the crowd, making no attempt to interact. She sobbed uncontrollably. The tears shimmered on her chocolate skin and made her eyes glisten like glass. Delicate, wide, grief-stricken, her eyes displayed the emotion he expected to see in the other detective's daughter. Just as Jason wondered who she was, the outcast woman left without approaching either casket.

When he scanned the crowd a few minutes later, he noticed both women were gone as the bagpipers eased into "Danny Boy" to call the fallen men home.

Jason and his mother arrived home from the funeral. She sat in her husband's favorite, worn-leather armchair in a near-catatonic state and stared at one of their wedding photos on the mantle. Jason thought about sitting on the carpet at her feet, to comfort her with his nearness, but he knew better. When he'd tried to console her on their way home from the funeral, she'd ignored him.

He turned to leave, but a sharp *thwack*, followed by the scattering of broken glass, startled him. Jason knew the source without turning around. Next to the wedding picture was a photo of a recent family camping trip. In the photo, his father tended a roaring fire. When Jason turned, the picture was gone from the mantle. He shifted his gaze to his mother. The image had overwhelmed her. He understood. Even the mere memory of the photo stirred his emotions. He was unwilling to associate his father with any kind of fire. Not anymore. Despite empathizing with his mother, he resisted the urge to stay with her. He trekked upstairs, harping on the last conversation he and his father had.

Jason had been poised on the edge of his father's desk, toying with the various trinkets. "Dad, you've known for a long time that I want to follow in your footsteps. I don't see why you're making such a big deal of it now." He'd dusted off a crystal pyramid bearing a plaque for outstanding service and gently replaced it near a sterling silver fountain pen. He'd lowered his gaze to meet his father's warm, but cock-eyed, expression.

"Son, it's the same old thing. Every father wants his children to take advantage of opportunities he never had, that's all. You graduated high school two years ago. You've been working, taking classes. Your mom and I have been saving. All I'm saying is it's time you pick a solid direction."

Tears streamed from Jason's eyes as he recalled how the rational discussion had quickly elevated into something more. Their baritone voices had carried throughout the house as they argued.

The fight had culminated in Jason screaming, "I can do whatever I want with *my* life!" He took a breath and puffed out his chest before adding, "You should be happy I even *want* to be like you! It's not like you're ever home with us. Maybe I don't wanna be like you at all. Maybe I just want to show you that it *is* possible to be a cop and a father in the same lifetime!"

Jason opened the door to his father's study, his fingers lingering on the doorknob. That day, Jason had slammed it with such force the frame shook. Several pictures had fallen from the walls, clattering to the floor.

Jason stood in the same spot in his father's tiny office, sobbing, surrounded by reminders of their argument. Broken glass in the wastebasket. Fractured frames picked up and placed on the shelves. The remaining plaques and framed newspaper articles served as a mounted cemetery of his father's esteemed career. With the setting sun filtering through the open drapes, the frames cast stretching shadows across the walls, like those of the headstones at the cemetery hours earlier.

Jason glanced at his father's desk and the most prominent headstone of all: a custom wooden lock-box containing a replica badge and his original service weapon. His father, an old-school cop, favored revolvers. The Colt Python .357 sat snugly in the blue velvet nest of the lock-box. Jason couldn't bring himself to touch it, to defile it with his intentions. He wanted to reach out and glide his fingers over the barrel's grooves and notches, the textured wooden grip of the handle.

Instead, he opened the top drawer. Nestled among the pens and paper clips was another, smaller revolver: a Colt Cobra .38. It resembled the commemorative one, but it had a stubbier barrel. Jason removed it. It felt cool, but heavier than he remembered. Loaded. Jason had never held a loaded gun before. Though he'd often nagged his father to take him to the shooting range, his father never found the time. But he'd taught Jason how to use this particular gun, in case he had to protect his mother. His father had always unloaded it first. Now the added weight paralleled his heavy decision.

He couldn't wait any longer.

Jason cocked the hammer. His father's soothing instructions played in his head, step by step.

Keep your finger off the trigger until you have made a conscious decision to shoot.

Jason gulped and placed his index finger inside the trigger guard and onto the trigger.

Be sure of your target and everything in your line of fire.

Jason shifted his gaze to the wall on his left. Nothing of consequence was on the other side.

Press, don't pull. Squeeze until you feel resistance.

Jason pulled the trigger.

At the last second, he flinched. Just a flicker of indecision, but it was too late. His blood sprayed the walls. The gun clanged to the floor. Jason's body crumpled. In the end, he laid in front of the door he had last slammed in his father's face.

Jason awoke to bright fluorescent lights and the smell of bleach, pine, and general sterility. A nurse scurried about his bedside. Her dark hair and eyes were somewhat familiar. That was all he could see through the haze. *Why is there a haze?* Suddenly, he was aware he wasn't wearing contact lenses. The woman greeted him cheerfully. He moaned an unintelligible response and looked around.

Jason eyed a roll-away bed tray to his right and a thick curtain divider beyond it. A cacophony of beeping and whirring fell on his ears. Jason realized he was lying in a hospital room. On his left, his mother dozed in one of two orange, plastic chairs near the window. Jason thought it was odd that his mother was asleep.

"Excuse me, nurse? How long have I been here?" Jason's voice startled him. It didn't sound like his, and the words themselves didn't sound right. His throat felt like he'd just eaten an entire pack of saltines. The dark-haired woman must have noticed the croak to his voice. She hurried out of the room and returned in a minute with a ridged, plastic cup full of ice chips. *What a beautiful woman.* A familiar beautiful. *Where have I seen her before?*

"Doctor," his mother corrected, apparently awakened by her son's voice. She rushed to his side with a broad smile and misty eyes.

"Huh?"

"She's a doctor, not a nurse." She brushed Jason's curls back soothingly, careful to avoid the bandages. She looked haggard and sleep-deprived. An image of her with messy hair and teary eyes flashed across Jason's mind, but he couldn't recall anything else about the image. It felt recent. *But what is recent?* He didn't even know what had happened that brought him there.

"Sorry, I guess that sounded sexist." Jason felt his cheeks flush but forced a smile.

"And I didn't raise you like that," his mother chided. She returned to the ugly orange chair and stretched. The chair squeaked in protest.

"It's okay," the dark-haired woman said with a chuckle. She fluttered around him, checking monitors and jotting readings down on a clipboard. Jason tried to read the name on her lab coat, but she moved too fast. He could barely focus his eyes.

"I'm just a resident," she continued. "And to answer your question, you've been here for"—she paused uncomfortably for a few seconds—"several days."

Her hesitation unnerved him. He watched her set the clipboard down and waited for her to elaborate. Instead, she reached into the plastic cup and placed an ice chip in his mouth. Her fingers glanced against his bottom lip. Suddenly hot, Jason appreciated the ice.

"What happened?" Jason's voice already felt foreign, as if he was speaking with a bucket on his head. Juggling the ice chip garbled his speech further. Frustrated, he moved to rub his forehead. Raising his hand took great effort, and it immediately met the soft roughness of gauze bandages.

Jason's face contorted in confusion. "What happened to me?" he demanded again, his voice frantic as he probed his head for answers. He tried to sit up, but his movements were sluggish and IVs tugged at his arms.

"Calm down, kid. You beat the odds. That's what happened." The doctor checked the lines in his arms, making sure they were still securely attached. "But I think I should let your mom explain the rest. Can I get you anything?"

"No, thanks," Jason answered, anxious to be alone with his mother and find out what had happened to him.

"No, thank you, *doctor*," his mother corrected again, on cue.

"Well, Jason, you're going to be transferred to our inpatient rehab center soon. If I don't see you again, have a speedy recovery. And if I do see you again, please call me Lyla."

The dark-haired doctor left Jason's hospital room. His mother left her orange chair and perched on the edge of his bed to stroke his brown curls again. He stared at her, wide-eyed and awaiting her explanation, grateful the chirping machines prevented a maddening silence.

"Jason, sweetheart," she said finally, "you had an accident."

"I know that, Mom. What kind of accident? Please, you're scaring me. Was I driving? Where's Dad?"

His mother swallowed hard, and her eyes blinked back tears. "Your father was killed, remember? Trying to save another detective from his burning home."

She waited while Jason processed the information for a second time. He vaguely remembered the solemn detectives delivering the news. Perhaps that's where the image of her, disheveled and crying, had originated. He said nothing but strained to remember more.

"After the funeral, you..." Her voice trailed off. Tears overwhelmed them both.

"What, Mom? Please." Jason wrestled with the IVs to reach for her hand. He squeezed it, imploring her to continue.

"You were in your father's office, with his...things...and accidentally shot yourself. The doctors gave a fancier explanation, but basically, the bullet penetrated your skull. Fortunately, it did minimal damage. Thank God for that." She crossed herself. Jason had only ever seen her do that when speaking of the dead. Then it hit him: he had almost died. *But what was I doing in my father's office? With my father's gun?*

"It was an...accident?" he asked.

"I was sitting downstairs when I heard the gunshot. I ran

upstairs, and there you were, blood everywhere. Your father's revolver was on the floor." She shielded her eyes from him. "It was an accident, Jason. I found you, and I thought I'd lost you too, but it was just an accident."

The chairs weren't orange.

Jason couldn't believe how something so small, something he felt so sure of, could be so wrong. He stared at the card in front of him. Dots. Lots of colored dots. According to the occupational therapist holding the card, a number was hidden in there somewhere, but he couldn't see it. Then again, he'd also thought that the visitors' chairs in his hospital room were orange, not blue. The confusion was a product of the bullet's path. The doctors said it traveled beneath the bony calvarium, around the circumference of his skull, and nicked his occipital lobe prior to its exit. Luckily, the bullet had avoided all his major blood vessels and only partially affected the portion of the brain responsible for sight and color perception.

"Apparently I'm missing more than just my contacts," he chuckled.

The therapist didn't laugh. She just pointed at the card again with earnest.

"I'm sorry, I don't see anything."

She grunted and flipped to a different card. More dots. Jason sighed with exasperation and let his eyes wander over her shoulder instead of undertaking the task before him. He spotted a burly, dark-skinned man with gray hair and a matching goatee. He stared straight at Jason. *Is he one of the hallucinations the doctors warned me about?* The man nodded and walked away, leaving Jason to turn down yet another card full of dots.

When Jason's session concluded, the therapist brought him back to his room. The inpatient rehab facility was separate from the hospital, but one could hardly tell the difference between the two. Residency rooms lined the halls. A hub of connected counters with people buzzing about stood in the center of each floor. Jason still slept on a hospital bed, the thin mattress lumpy from previous patients, but after just a few days, it showed signs of conforming to his frame. He looked forward to being helped into his room's faux-leather armchair, which could be quite comfortable with a few added pillows, but from the doorway, he saw that seat was already occupied.

He's waiting for me? Jason peered over at the therapist, who had guided him through the halls after his session. Though mentally and physically exhausted, the staff still forced him to walk as part of his rehab. He watched her eyes and swallowed his anxiety when she acknowledged the seated man with a smile. Jason hadn't imagined him after all.

Upon Jason's entry, the man stood and sat on one of the not-orange visitors' chairs. "How ya doin', son?" he asked after Jason settled into the armchair. It was uncomfortably warm after holding the large man who reached out a hand made of tree roots. "My name is Chief Albert Tunney. I worked—"

"With my dad," Jason finished.

"Yes. When I checked up on your mom the other day, she mentioned that you toyed with the idea of being a cop. Like your dad."

Right to business. Jason turned to the window. In the last couple of days, he'd regained flashes of memories of being in his dad's study, of their last encounter. He felt no desire to discuss any of it with his father's boss.

"I'm very sorry for your loss, Junior—"

"No one calls me that," Jason said harshly.

"I'm sorry. Your dad always called you that. Ya know, around the station."

"Not to my face," Jason spat. The doctors said he might experience inappropriate irritability, but he could swear he felt genuinely angry.

"Because he knew you hated it." Chief Tunney leaned forward, his interlaced fingers hanging between his knees. "He loved you very much, Jason. He was a good man and...Well, quite frankly, I would be honored to help you in any way I can. That is, if you still want to become a cop."

Jason slowly turned his head from the window and studied the man. His eyes were kind, but they were buried beneath his sturdy, authoritative demeanor. Jason realized that, outside of a full recovery, he hadn't thought about what he wanted to do. No matter what, his future depended on his present.

"With all due respect, Chief Tunney, what good am I to the force like this?" Jason extended his arms to indicate his surroundings. "My vision's blurry. I can't tell orange from blue or yellow from red. My speech only became clear a few days ago. I'm tired all the time. They say I might hallucinate. Hell, I thought *you* were a figment of my imagination when I saw you outside of my occupational therapy session."

The chief nodded, taking in the young man's concerns before responding. "I talked to your mom. You know what else *they* say? *They* say all of those issues are temporary."

Jason turned to the window again. "What if they're wrong?"

"What if they're not? Just think about it. I brought some material for you." He reached over to the other plastic chair and retrieved a stack of manuals and forms. "Look it all over. Study it if you're so inclined. When you get out of here, you'll be a few months shy of 21, right? I'll find out the test schedule. But first I need to know one thing."

"What's that?" Jason asked, still devoted to the view outside the window.

The chief barely needed to stretch his lengthy arm to place a hand on Jason's knee. "I need to know you didn't turn that gun, your father's gun, on yourself and pull the trigger. Your mom says it was an accident, and that's the official report, but I need to hear it from you."

Jason wanted to turn away from the window. He wanted to look the man in the eye, but he couldn't. The truth was, he didn't remember shooting himself. But something about the way his mother had described what happened, something about the way she uttered the word "accident," stayed with him. She must have known it rang false because she'd avoided meeting Jason's eye, just like he was averting his eyes from Chief Tunney.

"Chief, quite honestly, I don't remember even touching the gun. I've only in the last few days remembered coming home from the funeral and going to my father's study. I'm sorry, but I can't tell you what you want, or rather, what you need, to hear."

"Well then I guess your mother's word will have to be good enough for me. Take care, son. My card's in that stack somewhere. Use it if you need to."

5

She Chose Life.

LYLA STARED AT the fragile child lying on the table. When the paramedics had swarmed in with the small girl on the gurney, she froze. Only after hearing her name shouted several times did she remember it was her E.R. rotation and they expected her to jump in.

The girl had fallen and needed emergency surgery to repair a compound fracture in her fibula. She was only seven years old, with straw-blonde hair like Lyla's mother. The surgical team was preparing to sew up the incision.

Lyla had seen countless patients, but the little girl was by far the youngest Lyla'd ever seen opened up on the table. She'd calmed herself while she scrubbed in by breathing slowly in, then out, preparing herself for the tiny limbs and delicate vessels still developing in the innocent, prepubescent girl. With the procedure over, the entire team fell silent, satisfied the girl would soon see her eighth birthday.

Until she stopped breathing.

The calm and relief in the operating room disappeared in a cacophony of shouted inquiries and demands.

"Check her airway."

"It's clear."

"Get the scope!"

The shouts almost overlapped each other, and Lyla struggled to piece together where each voice originated from. The task was exacerbated by the blue surgical masks strapped to everyone's faces.

"Laryngospasms. She's reacting to the anesthesia. I can't intubate," the nurse anesthesiologist called. She moved aside the oxygen mask and struggled with the scope and E.T. tube at the girl's head.

Lyla snapped into action, determined not be frozen twice in one shift. She scoured her knowledge, trying to remember the protocol for a patient's throat spasming during surgery. She grabbed a vial of Anectine from the cart and injected it into the child's IV line with shaky hands. It was the same drug she'd injected her father with, right before she set him on fire. Funny how now it would save a girl's life by paralyzing her throat muscles to allow for intubation and artificial ventilation.

But it wasn't working.

"She's crashing," the nurse exclaimed.

The team fluttered around, launched into a type of coordinated dance—with Lyla hopelessly out of step. It was her first Code Blue in the operating room. With the patient so small, so fragile, the stakes were so grave.

"Doctor Kyle, what did you give her?" the lead surgeon demanded.

Lyla searched her brain for her mistake. Finding none, she answered confidently, "Anectine."

"Pulse and B.P. are dropping...fast!" the nurse called.

"Doctor Kyle, this patient has muscular dystrophy! She'll go into cardiac arrest!" the surgeon yelled, betraying his exasperation for only a moment.

"We're losing her!" the nurse cried.

The lead doctor interrupted his scolding to compose himself and take charge of the room. "Start C.P.R. Push an amp of calcium and an amp of bicarbonate first. Then push fifty-percent dextrose with ten units of insulin. Hyperventilate her! Now!"

"We're losing her!" Lyla repeated, half-expecting judgmental glares from her colleagues. After all, she was responsible. She stepped back, her head reeling. She watched the nurse anesthesiologist slide the tube into the girl's throat. At least her near-fatal error had relaxed the muscles in the girl's throat, easing the spasms.

"No, we are not!" the lead surgeon declared. He watched the anesthesiologist firmly attach the bag. The nurse rhythmically squeezed breaths into the girl's lungs. His team's confidence rose steadily with the girl's blood pressure.

They didn't lose her. But they almost had.

Once the girl became stable, the team filed out of the operating room. Everyone patted Lyla on the back, trying to convince her it was an honest mistake. Their faces were still covered with masks, but their eyes revealed their true emotion: pity. Lyla thought she detected a slight shake of the nurse's head, as if to say, "*Such a shame. The girl who had lost both parents in the space of one week now almost killed a child.*"

Maybe they were right. Lyla could no longer ignore the conversations that screeched to a halt as soon as she entered the break area or the locker room. The whispered re-tellings of her story flooding the hallways gnawed at her. Perhaps her grief *was* a liability. Or maybe the truth remained in the thought she'd had as she flicked her lighter before igniting her home: Death was her story.

Lyla wandered through the halls of the hospital, stopping to inspect details she may never see again: donated sculptures, portraits of benefactors, the brass trim of the elevators. She couldn't believe how quickly her last day of residency at West Philly Gen had arrived. Not because she had completed the program, but because she'd almost killed a child, almost stopped her heart cold, almost kept the young girl from seeing her eighth birthday.

Lyla had finally conceded to herself that she'd administered the drug while distracted over the fact she'd used the same drug to keep her father motionless before smothering him with flames. Seven days ago, the admission prompted her to request release from her residency.

The decision to leave turned out to be easier than Lyla anticipated. With both her parents gone and her childhood home diminished to ashes and the arson investigation still ongoing, perhaps the time had come to admit she didn't belong in medicine then—or ever. She was surprised she hadn't endangered a patient earlier.

Lyla rounded the corner to a hallway lined with historic artwork of Philadelphia General Hospital. Built in the early twentieth century and closed down in 1977, the illustrations portrayed the areas the current West Philly Gen shared with its predecessor. Lyla studied the painted and hand-drawn likenesses behind the glass display case, mesmerized by the many life cycles of the area. She wondered about the future of her childhood home, what would become of the blackened plot, when her clamshell phone clipped to her hip vibrated. She glanced at the caller I.D. It was her boyfriend, Anthony. Third time that day. With an eye roll and an exaggerated sigh, Lyla dismissed the call. Lately, Anthony had added to her inner conflict by bombarding her with constant questions. *Are you okay? Do you need anything? Do you want to talk?*

He meant well, certainly, but Lyla couldn't bear it anymore. Each of his reassurances served as constant reminders of the whole unfortunate chain of events. Her mother had killed herself. Because of her father. So she'd killed her father. Lyla needed time and space to accept those life-altering incidents. Privately.

Not only did Lyla want the investigation to conclude so she could rebuild her life, but perhaps she could also rebuild her home—her own version of the ever-evolving Philadelphia General Hospital. Lyla smiled briefly before her gaze wandered from the old hospital to her reflection in the glass. More specifically, to the maize-yellow shirt peeking out from under the collar of her blue scrubs. When she'd put it on that morning, she'd noticed a few tiny specks of acrylic paint on the right sleeve.

Lyla regretted not taking some of her mother's artwork the night of the fire. It was a shame they wouldn't have fit into her bag. But maybe Lyla could dabble in art—something her mom had always encouraged—as part of her new life, a way to pay homage to her mother. Ever since she was a young girl, her mother had admired Lyla's creative side and said she possessed an uncanny eye and talent to match. Lyla couldn't escape the feeling she should do something else to please her mother, as if she was *meant* to do something else. She felt torn between the bereavement of losing her mother and the empowerment of killing her father. Perhaps killing her father wasn't enough. Regardless, she needed time to figure it all out.

But with Anthony hovering and recently talking about marriage, how could Lyla figure anything out? She supposed she loved him, but they had only been seeing each other for a year, and even that time was off and on. Plus, how could she think of marriage after finding out what a sham her own parents' union turned out to be? Layer upon layer of lies, infidelity, and lost love. Or perhaps love still lingered there somewhere, beneath all the resentment and bitterness. Bottom line, Lyla had no intention of marrying Anthony—or anyone else. She couldn't bear to repeat her mother's mistakes.

Lyla headed back up several floors, to the locker room. Though she hadn't expected fanfare, in her heart, she wanted it. Disappointment enshrouded her when she made her rounds of goodbyes instead of patient check-ins. Even more so when no one steered her toward a break room filled to the brim with balloons and the scent of buttercream-frosted cake. Instead, she emptied her locker in solitude and silence.

The metal hinges on her locker screeched. Lyla bundled all of her spare scrubs into a single sweatshirt and dumped it into a cardboard box she'd grabbed from supply. It wasn't nearly as large as the one she'd taken to hide the discarded vials bin last week. As she shut her locker for the last time, precariously balancing the cardboard box on her raised knee and her large tote bag on her shoulder, she heard CJ's shuffling gait. She turned, and a wave of her dark hair fell into her eyes as her mouth turned up into a grin. She should have known CJ wouldn't let her down. The squirrelly, acne-peppered kid swapped her heavy box for a bouquet of multi-colored Gerbera daisies with several balloons tethered to it, dancing above their heads.

"Hey, Lye-Dye, how was your last day?" he asked cheerfully, his hand grazing hers as he grabbed her tote bag.

"You know I hate it when you call me that." She poked his chest hard, but still playfully. "As for my last day, I'm feeling quite indifferent about it." She paused before mumbling, "So is everyone else, apparently." She wove through the locker room, threading between alternating rows of benches and stacked lockers.

"Why indifferent?" His free arm wrapped around her shoulders, his voice and touch soothing her as they walked toward the locker room's swinging door.

Lyla shrugged. "No one really seemed to care."

"Well you're dropping out of medical residency, Lyla. You won't tell anyone why. All anyone can assume is that it's because of your parents." CJ stopped short of the exit, placed the box and bag on a bench, and took her hands. His blue eyes were round and bulging, almost cartoonish. He examined her intently. "Has it occurred to you no one knows quite what to say?"

"I guess you're right." Lyla swallowed hard and sniffed back tears she knew CJ would eagerly wipe away if she allowed them to fall. "What are you doing right now?"

CJ raised an eyebrow. "Cheering you up?"

"You hungry?" she asked.

"Starved."

Lyla's smile trembled as she shoved the locker room door open.

Though the beginning of September meant the start of the fall semester, the food trucks lining the curbs only stuck around until late afternoon. CJ and Lyla walked arm in arm to a local cheesesteak place, grabbed some dinner, and brought it back to campus to eat. They chose the same spot they always chose: a grassy hill beneath a stand of maple trees. The leaves rustled as CJ and Lyla nestled into the plush grass. They both inched to and fro and left to right, trying to avoid the reflection of the setting sun in the surrounding buildings. The orange blaze caused them to squint until they found the perfect angle.

Lyla nibbled a bite of her cheesesteak before her eyes welled up and her lower lip quivered, but not from the motion of chewing. "I quit because I almost killed a little girl," she blurted out, almost involuntarily.

CJ placed his sandwich down on its crinkled aluminum wrapper and shifted so he sat beside Lyla rather than across from her. He folded his right arm around her and used his free hand to guide her face toward him with a gentle, crooked finger beneath her chin. Lyla sobbed, drowning out her friend's cooing and hushing.

"You know I hate it when you cry, Lye-Dye."

"I know," she managed to sniff out, her voice croaking as she looked away.

"Do you want to talk about it?" he coaxed.

Lyla told CJ about the seven-year-old girl slowly, like molasses from a carafe. She awaited harsh criticism and judgmental chiding, but it never came. When she finished, puffy-eyed and sniveling, CJ brought her face to him again and said simply, "Mistakes happen, sweetheart."

Lyla glowered at him. *How dare he proffer such a clichéd response.* She felt the temperature rise in her cheeks.

But CJ continued, his eyes distant like a faraway, storm-tossed sea. "I almost died once, too, you know. My parents tell me that when I was a kid, my regular babysitter had an emergency and sent over a friend to care for me in her place. The girl was in a rush, and my parents were running late for their show. Everyone forgot to tell the replacement that I had a severe peanut allergy." Lyla gazed at him, her stare milder; he had her attention. "Well, when I got hungry that night, the babysitter fished some of my dad's orange-looking peanut butter crackers from the top cabinet in the kitchen to tide me over until dinnertime. I was only a toddler, didn't know what they were, and I started eating them. Immediately my mouth itched and my throat closed. I couldn't breathe. I vaguely remember that part, that desperate feeling of fighting for air, helplessly knowing your body is failing you. I knew where my mother kept my EpiPen and tried to lead the babysitter to the bathroom, but she just ran around, panicked. She called 911, and I lost consciousness right as the paramedics arrived. It was one of the rare occasions where an emergency tracheotomy was necessary." He rolled his eyes, presumably at his shitty luck. "I woke up in the hospital with a hole in my neck."

"Wow," Lyla said, engrossed. CJ tugged at his shirt collar, revealing the scar on his throat. She touched the irregular splotch of stretched skin in the center of his collar bone, surprised she'd never noticed it.

"Yeah, but the moral of the story, Lye-dye, is my parents forgave my regular babysitter and her friend. And so did I. Because things happen. Mistakes happen. Even the almighty doctors at West Philly Gen are human. Do you think you're the first person to almost kill a patient? If you were, malpractice lawyers might have to collect unemployment."

Lyla chuckled. She already felt better, and soon the conversation lightened to the normal hospital staff gossip. Then he asked about Anthony, the same question he always asked. "So, how's Anthony...doing?" Each time, he asked it the same way, with a lingering pause after her boyfriend's name. Lyla knew he hoped she would reveal they'd broken up.

"He's fine. Concerned for me."

"As he should be."

"Yeah, well, I'm kinda drowning in his concern, choking on it even. And now he's blabbering on about marriage, and I just can't think about that. I don't even think I want to get married after what happened to my mom."

Lyla felt dark with melancholy again. But CJ delivered, as he always did. He calmed her with his humble stuttering and general boy-next-door affability. CJ knew how to appeal to her competitive side, the side of her that always had something to prove.

"Don't you want to be better than your folks?" he asked. "Don't you want to be different? Any normal person would swear off marriage, but a strong person would overcome those fears. Fall in love. Have the picture-perfect life that they deserved, that *you* deserve."

CJ placed a hand on Lyla's knee. His eyes were wide as they sat together in the grass, cheesesteaks neglected and cooling. She stared into his eyes. They pleaded with her, as though if she listened close enough, she'd hear him follow up with, "the life that *we* deserve." She knew that's what her friend really meant.

"You're right, I know you're right," Lyla finally conceded. "I guess only time will tell."

Lyla playfully fondled his thin, dirty-blond hair, ignoring the glimmer in his eyes. But with each passing breath, he drew nearer and she hoped he intended only to share body heat.

Night fell and CJ insisted on escorting Lyla home, even though it required two trains and a bus. They spent the end of the journey on a double-bus: two regular-sized buses joined in the center by a section resembling an accordion.

Lyla jumped at the chance to drag CJ to the seats in the swiveling center, giggling as though they were riding a carnival Tilt-a-Whirl. With every rolling shift, her troubles felt further away. No dead parents. No near-fatal mistake in the operating room. No apprehensions about life or marriage for a solid thirty minutes.

When the bus screeched to a standstill at their stop, Lyla and CJ spilled out from the rear doors, dizzy from their trip and drunk from laughter. They tumbled along the sidewalk for several blocks, their arms intertwined like a pretzel. The headlights of passing cars streaked their faces and lit their way.

What little survived of Lyla's home lay a block ahead on their right, just peeking into view. The house had been reduced to a pile of blackened rubble with charred beams jutting about in every direction—an enormous, sooty bird's nest. As they approached the scorched and shriveled remains, a thin gasp escaped CJ's lips. Lyla knew he had tried to restrain it and failed.

"That's right, you haven't seen it since the fire," Lyla said softly.

"No. Lyla, I'm so sorry." He grabbed her hand and squeezed it as they drew closer.

"It's okay. I mean, it's been tough, don't get me wrong, but I think I made the right decision to stay at my neighbors' house while they're in Florida. They've been really generous, and it allows me to stay close to things." *This way I can keep tabs on the investigation.*

"Yeah, it was lucky for you they were heading down for the winter right when you needed a place to crash."

She stared at him until he realized his gaffe: Lyla was in no way lucky. He lowered his eyes and squeezed her hand again, an apology she accepted.

"So, the insurance is covering everything?" CJ asked awkwardly, stumbling to change the subject.

"Yeah, the insurance plus both life-insurance policies. I'm sure I could have bought a house and lived off the rest for quite a while, but it was more important for me to rebuild *this* house. I'm told the fire investigation could take several more months though."

"Yikes."

They both came to a dead stop, not at the full sight of the burnt-down home—they had managed not to gawk as they passed it in silence—but at the neighbor's house. The back porch, and most of the yard, glowed. They were illuminated by candles, string lights, and white paper bag luminaries— brilliant, twinkling white stars, brought down from the Cosmos to the Earth.

It was so beautiful, Lyla felt herself crying in a way she hadn't in a long time: tears of joy. Despite the blur of her moist eyes, she saw Anthony kneeling in the center of it all. Tall, broad shoulders without being stocky. Same dark hair as Lyla. The green in his eyes sparkled almost as brightly as the decor. He caught Lyla's gaze. The shadows sculpted both of their faces, making them appear like a matching pair of figurines atop their own wedding cake.

Anthony, either oblivious or apathetic to CJ's presence, shouted, "Lyla Kyle, will you marry me?" He beamed almost as brightly as the yard. Almost as brightly as the diamond in his hand.

Lyla shook her head slowly in disbelief. But disbelief soon turned to freedom. With each subtle, side-to-side movement, her mind broke free of the shackles of the past few days. It broke free from the grief, the uncertainty, and the death. She chose love and a leap of faith. She chose life.

Lyla ran to him, her long legs eating up the distance in a handful of strides. With her fears abated by her talk with CJ, she fell to her knees in front of Anthony with tears streaming down her cheeks. She grasped his face and kissed him. Hard. Heavily. When she pulled back, her voice cracked as she said, "I choose you." Lyla breathed in a gulp of crisp air, as though she could inhale the twinkling lights and capture them within her heart. "I choose a life with you, Anthony."

"Is that a yes?"

Without waiting for confirmation, perhaps not needing it, Anthony put the ring on Lyla's trembling left hand and they embraced. He kissed her neck, and the tickling sensation that followed left them falling to the ground, rolling around in laughter and tears. Their joy rang louder still when they bumped into a luminary, almost setting a fire in their excitement.

Neither noticed as CJ sank back into the shadows, beyond the glowing lights and joy, to wait for the bus that would bring him back to the other side of Philadelphia.

6
An Insect on Display.

LYLA WAITED. Only a few months had passed since their courthouse wedding, but Lyla had already noticed the signs. The showers as soon as he came home from yet another late night. The new clothes that went straight to the dry-cleaner; Lyla could easily speculate what they were stained with. She wondered if her mother had seen the signs, too. Had she ignored them or just been naive, blind to their true effect on her? Lyla imagined the little white lies as tiny cracks in a snowy hillside growing into larger, more transparent lies that could bury a whole town in a tumbling avalanche of dishonesty. That town had once been Lyla's mother, and now it was Lyla.

That day, the phone rang. She answered it. Her first hang-up phone call. So she waited, eerily calm. She waited for Anthony to come home and wave to her absentmindedly before bypassing her to go upstairs, which had become their frigid ritual. She sipped her chai tea and waited for him to take a shower and return downstairs. In the center seat of their sofa, arms outstretched across the back, legs crossed at the ankles, feet resting on the glass coffee table with the jagged driftwood base, Lyla waited.

Anthony lightly jogged downstairs. His wet hair dampened his shirt collar. He was still fumbling with the buttons as he entered the room, his glistening chest disappearing inch by inch. He was handsome. Just like her father. In more ways than one.

"Did you get her scent off?" Lyla asked calmly. She knew it came across as far more frightening than shouting. Anthony's mouth opened, caught in amazement and wonder. She put a finger to her chin, mocking thoughtfulness, before she added, "I think I still smell her. Maybe you should try more cologne."

"You smell my secretary?" he said with a laugh that sounded forced. Anthony rounded the love seat to sit across from her. She imagined his mind squirming. His eyes betrayed him. "I told Edna not to hug me. I'm not that great of a boss."

"Please don't try to diffuse the situation with a joke. I know what you're doing." Lyla removed her feet from the coffee table, planted them on the floor, and pressed forward like a predator closing in on its prey. In a hushed tone, she said, "Besides, your secretary called out sick today. And *you* never returned to the office after you left for lunch. You forget, I have your law firm on speed dial, my love."

Anthony didn't speak. He rose from the love seat and strolled around it, placing a barrier between himself and his accuser, as liars often did. Lyla still smiled sweetly when he faced her. His body stiffened, rigid arms hanging at his sides. "I had errands to run."

"So her name is 'Erin?'" Lyla said with a sly smile, trying not to enjoy herself.

"No, her name is not 'Erin.' She doesn't have a name. There is no *her*, there is no *she*. God, Lyla, you're so paranoid! Paranoid about us becoming your parents. You should really see someone or something."

Lyla could not count how many times her husband rolled his eyes in an effort to avoid her glare. She chuckled. A laugh of pity, most definitely. She was trying to decide whether she pitied herself or Anthony when his cell phone rang. Lyla lunged for the vibrating phone on the coffee table. Her delicate, red bone china teacup tilted on its saucer and spilled cooled chai onto the cream-colored carpet. Though they scratched at each other's hands, Lyla managed to grab the phone first and answer it.

Lyla kept her husband at bay with her free arm extended, blocking him as he swung wildly to snatch the phone from her. She heard a high-pitched, yet sultry voice echo "Hello" several times before hanging up. Lyla imagined the phone call her mother had received the night before her death while her father sat smugly at the dinner table. Just like Anthony stood smugly before her now.

Lyla opened her mouth to say something, but her rage took the form of momentum—strength and power, not words—and she shoved her husband with all her might. Caught off guard, Anthony's eyes widened, and he lost his balance. He teetered and fell backward onto the coffee table.

Lyla watched her husband's descent for what felt like an entire minute, as if he fell from a much higher distance, as if each body part was in its own separate free fall. She held his gaze, feeding on the fear and horror in his pupils. Glass exploded around them and still Lyla stared him down. The branches of the driftwood base impaled him. Shooting toward Lyla through Anthony's torso, they reached for her, raised in genuflection.

Anthony lay there, pinned like an insect on display, as he tried to wriggle free, flailing his arms and legs. Blood erupted from his mouth and nose, rolled down his face, pooled in the crook of his neck, and seeped steadily into his shirt. Lyla wanted to stomp on his chest. Fury smoldered within her, itching to drive the wooden stakes of revenge deeper into his cheating heart.

Lyla was shocked by those feelings at first, but she soon found herself basking in the blazing empowerment that grew within her. Its warmth spread from her gut out to her limbs and into the tips of her fingers and toes. Just like the night she lit the fire that burned down her childhood home. Lyla understood: That fire would stay with her forever. Death truly was her story.

Lyla poured herself a glass of Bordeaux. She sipped it, wishing she could watch Anthony rot. Instead, she called the police after summoning fraudulent tears, another similarity to the night of the house fire. As she recited her address to the operator between sniffles, Lyla couldn't help but wonder if some people lived their whole lives without ever calling 911. Then she found herself amused by the fact that two of the three times she had done so was the result of her own doing.

Lyla toasted her husband's blood-drained body with a soft chuckle and gulped down the last of her wine.

7

A Sea of Names Etched in Stones.

JILLIAN SAT ON her bed and focused her longing gaze out of her bedroom window. She had mostly stayed in her apartment for six months, watching the trees change from golden leaves to snow-laden branches. From late sunsets to early darkness. The melting snow provided an audible crackle, ironically similar to a fire. But such comparisons only served to remind Jillian that she needed to get out of the house for more than just food and doctor's visits.

She'd managed to earn a decent income writing articles from home for psychology publications such as *gradPSYCH* and *Psychology Today*. But sooner or later, she needed to put the past behind her, put the box of bloody keepsakes behind her. With spring fast approaching, Jillian could not fathom a better time to rise from the ashes. She chuckled at her clichéd desire and storybook plot of spring and rebirth and rising from the ashes. She was no Phoenix. She wasn't resolute or resilient. In fact, she was terrified. But the timing felt right.

Jillian shoved off the bed with some effort and crossed her bedroom. She pushed the box full of bloody clothes way back into the recesses of her closet—and her mind—and prepared to begin her new life. Jillian picked out a deep-purple suit and held it against the newfound convexity of her midsection. She hoped it would fit. The next day, she was applying for an open psychologist position at a Center City practice. But that day would be the first day she left the house out of more than sheer necessity. The first thing on her agenda: visit the grave of her fallen but not forgotten lover, Calvin Kyle. Pushing a box behind a pile of shoes wasn't closure enough to embark on the future.

Jillian strolled through the cemetery gates, blue sky above, stone-gray pavement below. The sun felt good and warmed her body beneath the woolen trench coat. As she abandoned the walkway in favor of the grass, weaving through the headstones, she realized how much she had missed the sun. Allowing her body and mind to bask in the warmth, Jillian thought about all the things she would do after finally putting the past behind her. She smiled— wondering if the practice she planned to join offered opportunities for partnership—as something tugged on her pant leg. She gasped. Broad daylight or not, it was still a cemetery, and cemeteries were eerie in any light.

She looked down to find her pant leg had simply snagged on the weeds sprouting from the base of a small headstone. Jillian bent to free herself and someone brushed past her, causing her heart to skip again. When she stood, she sighed with relief. A man, slightly younger than herself, had bumped into her. He had a rather odd haircut with a short, stubbly section above his right ear reaching around to the back of his head.

"Excuse me, I'm so sorry. I wasn't watching where I was going," he stammered. He glanced backward at a woman crossing the threshold of the iron gates before mumbling, "I thought I recognized her." When he turned, the sun highlighted the shaved area of his head, revealing his odd haircut was the result of a jagged, pink scar.

"No problem," Jillian said tersely. She continued to her

destination. Her voice sounded foreign to her ears; she hadn't spoken to anyone other than Mel in months. Even when she visited her doctor, she spoke very little. But as she neared her lover's gravestone, she felt the urge to speak to it. To speak to *him*. She would soon get used to hearing her voice again.

She unbuttoned her coat to sit next to the grave, but her pants dug into her expanded abdomen uncomfortably. Instead, she stood and looked down upon the stone. She opened her mouth to speak. Her unfamiliar voice did not follow. An overwhelming bout of nausea struck her, and she braced herself against Calvin—well, his stone, anyway.

The nausea passed, and Jillian sucked in some fresh winter air while she leaned against Calvin's headstone. She rubbed her swollen, upset belly and released the cold air, ready to begin again.

"I'm ready to move forward, Cal. I may have done a horrible thing, but it looks like I won't be held accountable for it just yet. I'm sorry for that, but I needed you to see me, to talk to me, one last time. I thought I could change your mind, but I see now I probably couldn't, no matter what the circumstances. I'm ready to move forward, but not entirely without you. A piece of you will always be with me, always in my life. I love you. Goodbye."

Jillian tucked her black hair behind both ears and leaned forward to kiss the gravestone. When she rose to her full height, she noticed a woman heading in her direction. Storming in her direction, in fact. Jillian recognized her as the lady who'd distracted the young stranger. Now that she was closer, Jillian also recognized her from the news: Calvin's daughter, Lyla.

Buttoning her coat around her pregnant stomach and

yanking the collar up around her chin, Jillian hurried off the way she came, soothing her unborn baby through the lining of her deep coat pockets.

Young Jason Brighthouse Jr. emerged from the outpatient facility, finally finished with physical therapy. He'd gone from his muscles quivering if he tried to sit upright for fifteen minutes to talking and walking normally.

"Just like a real boy," he said in a high-pitched whisper. He chuckled at the reference to his childhood favorite, *Pinocchio*. But Jason no longer felt stiff and awkward. Six weeks of rehab and three months of physical therapy had done away with that for good. The doctors said he might experience exaggerated fatigue, but outside of that, only a scar remained.

Chief Tunney had visited Jason in the hospital several times, inspiring him like his father had and encouraging him like his father had not. After much debate, Jason decided he would join the police force. He wanted to honor his father's life, not his wishes—or rather, his orders. Once committed to the idea, Jason gleefully pored over the stack of reading materials the Chief had left behind and anxiously filled out the Police Officer Recruit Application.

But something still nagged at him. The Chief had assured him he would pass the psych evaluation, as long as he was telling the truth about not remembering the accident, but Jason wasn't quite sure it *was* an accident. His mother said it was, but she didn't act like it. Nor did Jason feel like it was. But perhaps his memory loss was a blessing, allowing him to become a police officer. The taint of an attempted suicide would certainly prevent it.

Jason hailed a cab and tried not to focus too much on the

psych test. He'd been told he only needed to exceed expectations. He had done that. Tenfold. He felt stronger than he'd ever been, and tomorrow he would take his written competency test. But first, he needed to visit his father's grave and apologize for disobeying his orders.

Jason walked briskly to his father's plot. When he reached it, a small tattered flag stuck out of the ground, fluttering in the wind. Presidents Day had only just passed, but the elements had already assaulted the flag. Beside it lay a bundle of dead daisies whose dried petals jumped into the breeze one by one. He plopped down, sat cross-legged, and stared at the majestic stone before him. He traced his father's name—his namesake—with his index finger and spoke.

"I'm sorry, Dad. I won't apologize for the admiration I hold for you. I won't apologize because you were and always will be my idol. I won't apologize for wanting to be just a fraction of the man you were. It's not what you wanted for me, it's not college, but I promise, I will make you proud."

With that, Jason set a photocopy of his completed application before the headstone and stabbed the flag's little wooden staff through the paper, pinning it to the ground. He stood up and kissed the cold stone, feeling good about the life before him. On the way back to his car, he heard sobbing competing with the whistle of the wind in the bare tree branches. Jason wondered about the woman he'd accidentally run into earlier.

Jason searched the cemetery and soon located the source of the crying sitting on the ground against a tombstone: a young lady with dark hair, the one he'd thought recognized. She wore large sunglasses, and her dark hair swallowed the sunlight, reminding him of the woman he had seen at his father's funeral six months earlier. Perhaps that's why she looked familiar. She must have sensed his eyes because her head snapped up and she lifted her shades. The gaze she offered pierced him.

Last night, Lyla had finally done it. She sat up against the pillows on her bed. A mixture of disbelief and excitement made her shake with a borderline erotic tremble as she recalled the details of the previous night's festivities. Casually, the man had mentioned his wife. Just sprinkled that information in among civilized conversation. The smoldering coals that forever resided inside of her flared up.

Lyla's cheeks had burned. Flashes of her mother's bloodless, broken body emerged. Inwardly, she justified killing the man, her decision made without hesitation. She couldn't recall the rest of the date except for repeatedly checking the time, reading it upside-down on his wristwatch.

After dinner, Lyla and her date had walked arm-in-arm out to the parking lot. They had driven separate cars. Lyla pretended to scratch around in her purse for her keys as she pried open her mother's tortoise shell eyeglass case. She had removed the glasses long ago and filled it with syringes of the last of the succinylcholine she'd recovered from the hospital.

When the man had walked her to her car door, she drew him near with her left arm firmly around his waist. He leaned in for a goodnight kiss. Lyla kissed him back as she snaked her right arm up and around his neck. Seconds into the kiss, she felt his body jerk at the surprise of having been jabbed with a syringe. His body froze. Lyla glanced from left to right. No one around. She jumped in her car and pulled off before his body had time to hit the pavement.

She'd driven away with a newfound exuberance and slept soundly. In the clarity of a new day, it felt like a victory for her mother. Lyla had to tell her. She quickly dressed and headed for her mother's grave.

Lyla arrived and crept up the paved walkway through the towering, wrought-iron gates. Only a few living souls meandered among the deceased, and the phrase *silent as the grave* entered her mind. Emotions danced in her stomach as she neared her parents' plots. She hadn't visited since their funerals because she felt torn between her love for her mother and her contempt for her father.

But Lyla pressed on, partially frozen blades of grass crunching underfoot. When she looked up from the frost-covered ground, she noticed a woman huddled near her parents' graves. Lyla quickened her pace, but the woman scurried off at her approach.

"Hey! Hey, you! Get back here!" Lyla called, trotting through the grass in her high heels.

Lyla's failure to recognize the woman drew her stomach into her throat. The stranger had most likely come to visit her father's grave. One of *his girls*. Perhaps *the girl,* the one who had led her mother to her miserable end. Lyla furiously pursued the woman, threading between the headstones, ignoring the bare willow branches whipping at her cheeks, but the intruder had vanished. Lyla was left alone among a sea of names etched in stones.

Lyla panted, both from the chase and from her fury. Like a snorting bull, she stood hunched over in the center of the cemetery, eyes searching for her father's mistress. Seeing the woman reminded Lyla of the anger she still felt toward her father and husband. Not sadness—for she felt none—but the raw anger that fueled the power of it all. The power she'd felt last night.

She longed for that again. She craved it even then as she glanced from grave to grave, wondering if the men buried beneath them had been faithful or philandering. That wasn't the first time she found herself thinking such thoughts about men. Because of that, she no longer felt capable of living an ordinary life. Last night proved that something extraordinary pulled at her. At first, Lyla had found herself startled by the urge to kill the men who sat across from her at the candlelit tables and cozy booths of romantic restaurants. Now she knew better. Abandoning her pursuit, Lyla again headed for her mother's grave.

The late-winter chill had absorbed into her mother's headstone. When Lyla approached, the sight of her father's grave next to her mother's sickened her. He didn't deserve to be near her in death any more than he deserved to in life. Lyla turned her back on him, then she sat and inched backward to lean against her mother's stone.

She tried to imagine herself as a girl, leaning into her mother's arms after her nightly bath as her mother gently brushed her hair. In reality, the frost penetrated her clothes and reminded Lyla of her mother's lifeless body the day she'd found her. In that moment, the tears overcame her. She sat sobbing for what felt like an hour.

Sensing a presence, she sat erect, hoping someone had come to comfort her. She hoped for the spirit of her mom—a woman who had believed in such things. Disappointment set in when she saw a kid with a funny haircut staring at her from twenty yards away. Lyla knew he'd heard her crying and glowered at him for invading her intimate moment of vulnerability.

After snatching her sunglasses from the top of her head

and shoving them in her coat pocket, she wiped her face aggressively, chiding herself for her weakness. Resolute and composed, Lyla stood and boldly faced her father—his grave anyway—and spit on it. To her mother's stone, she whispered a defiant vow, one she'd come up with while driving away from her date's body last night.

"Don't worry, Mom, I'll get 'em. Every last one of them. I got one last night and..." Lyla straightened. Suddenly, she wished she had something to leave behind. Not flowers, but something to prove her allegiance to her mother. Each kill avenged her, one man at a time. Then something came to Lyla. She bent closer and whispered, "Next time, I'll paint you a better picture." With a wink, she walked off, still speaking. "Now if you'll excuse me, Mommy, I have a date tonight."

8

Blood in the Paint.

LYLA'S SLENDER FINGERS pried open the tortoise shell eyeglass case full of syringes. She removed the only one containing blood. She'd killed again last night, hours after visiting her parents' graves. Hours after seeing one of her father's hussies hovering over him, grieving someone who wasn't hers to grieve. Lyla had thought of that scene many times during her date. She thought of it again as her date toppled to the ground, and once again when she extracted a sample of his blood.

When she and her mother painted together, Lyla's favorite part was watching her mother mix the paint. She'd turn red and white into the perfect hue for a pink summer sunset. Susannah had known just what combination to use for the trees' reflection in the river or a sunflower coated with dew. Lyla would watch her magically create colors, stirring gently. Her tendons pulsed with each motion, almost in anticipation of the art to come.

In the center of her recently converted art studio, Lyla released the syringe's blood into a small, newly bought can of cadmium red paint. She tossed the syringe in a bag by the door. She would dispose of it more permanently later. Leaning over her desk, she spun a carousel full of paint brushes. Tall, lean shadows swirled across all four walls. When the brushes came to a standstill, like a beautiful, painter's bouquet, Lyla chose a slender, round brush with a wooden handle and rubber grip. She cradled the small can and adoringly stirred the blood in the paint.

Lyla had promised to paint her mother a better picture. What better image than the terror behind her victims' eyes? What better medium than their blood?

So Lyla rocked gently on her wooden stool. She wore her mother's favorite butter-yellow shirt, hummed her mother's favorite Beatles song, and painted her mother a pretty, terrifying picture.

Note from the Author: Now that you have finished *Blood in the Past*, won't you please consider leaving a review on the website from which you purchased your copy? Reviews are the best way for readers to discover up and coming authors, such as myself, and I would really appreciate it. Thank you.

Jordanna East

Jordanna East

About the Author

Jordanna East readily confesses that she started writing a novel one day when she was broke and unemployed. Her cable had been turned off. SHE WAS BORED. So she sat down on her bed and started writing...and she hasn't stopped. Though, now she has cable and pens her Psychological Thrillers at an actual desk. She lives with her husband in South Jersey and their two cats, both named after food.

Blood in the Past is the prelude novella to her debut *Blood for Blood Series*, which follows three lives entwined by deaths and consequences, revenge and obsession. The first full-length novel in the series, *Blood in the Paint*, will be released this winter. Also be on the lookout for *The Word and the Way*, a serialized novel revolving around a fanatical cult plagued by abusive and power hungry members, sexual abuse, and murder—and the young couple desperate to escape. Episode One of the series will be released in 2014.

Contact the Author

Jordanna East loves to hear from her fans. You can find her everywhere:

http://jordannaeast.com
http://www.facebook.com/JordannaEast
http://www.twitter.com/JordannaEast
https://www.plus.google.com/JordannaEast
http://www.goodreads.com/JordannaEast

Or email her directly:
jordannaeast@gmail.com

Acknowledgments

Bear with me while I grovel at the feet of a few people. I would like to thank my editor, Cassie Cox, of Red Adept Publishing Services. Working with her was invaluable. Kit Foster, of Kit Foster Designs, for designing my cover, my author logo, and my press logo. Thank you, Kit, for always dealing with my pickiness and nagging emails so graciously. Thank you to Karen Perkins, of LionheART, for her formatting services. I never could have done it myself. I would also like to thank my beta readers, Amanda Surowitz, Ileandra Young, Rhonda Ramsey, Tonya Kerrigan, Erin Lewis, and Courtney Moore for taking the time to read, critique, and point out major plot holes that I'm too embarrassed to even think about now. Thank you to Greg Johnston for looking over the opening scene that the betas didn't get a chance to see. A huge thank you to the members of the Crime Scene Writers group on Yahoo, specifically, Kelly Whitley, Melissa Maygrove, Lee Lofland, Wes Harris, and Wally Lind. They provided me with their experience and expertise in medico-legal procedures and even, on occasion, reviewed a few of my scenes. (And it goes without saying that any mistakes found are mine alone and are a result of my own misinterpretation of their facts.) And thank you too all the blog and social networking followers I've befriended over the last year and a half, those that have supported me, cheered me on, and featured me on their own websites. I hope I can repay the favor one day.

Thank you to my sister, Danae, my niece, D'vonnae, for their constant support and excitement. And for telling me how proud they are of me (And they should be. This was hard!). Thank you to my fantastic in-laws. Momma Lisa, Mr Rob, Courtney, & Dan, I really lucked out with you guys. Thank you to my friends who have supported me, asked me "How's the writing going?" and "When's the book coming out?" over and over again and never tiring of my answer ("Soon!").

And I saved the best and closest to my heart for last. My husband, Justin. I could write a separate book about his never-ending love and encouragement, but I'm not a romance writer, so he's stuck with this paragraph. I dedicated this book to my husband because without him it just wouldn't be. I would've quit and regretted it for the rest of my life. Not only that, Justin financed this little endeavor. I've had the privilege and luxury of writing full-time while he shouldered all the responsibilities and all the stress of running a household. That's how much he believed in me.